Games
People
Play

Games People Play

**A Serialized Novel by
Wesley Adams and Daphne McGee**

Book 6 of the Soap Opera Inspired Story Collection
Series Created by Gary Brin

Episodes 1-6

Cover photograph courtesy of www.pexels.com
Cover photograph was digitally enhanced and visually altered for this edition.
Cover design and book layout © 2021 by Standish Press

FIRST EDITION

Copyright © 2021 by Standish Press

For more information about reprint rights please visit
www.standishpress.com

ISBN—978-1-945510-07-6

MANUFACTURED IN THE UNITED STATES OF AMERICA

Sometimes when you least expect it a chance meeting happens and changes history forever in ways never imagined.

An opportunity is what you make of it—though the end results aren't always what you wanted or expected.

Contents

Intro

Games People Play was inspired partly by the beloved classic novel *Treasure Island.* While several characters from Robert Louis Stevenson's masterpiece are mentioned in relation to present-day characters in this serialized story—this novel is not a direct sequel to Stevenson's novel. For the most part it could be considered a spinoff of sorts but not in the traditional sense. In addition to mentioning several characters from Stevenson's novel, several real-life historical events and people not part of the original storyline of *Treasure Island* was linked to his entertaining masterpiece as well for dramatic purposes only, and in no way should it be deemed Stevenson's idea or connected in any way to the fictional 1883 novel. Aspects of other novels were also thrown in for good measure as well when needed, most notably the classic 1930 novel *Maltese Falcon* by Dashiell Hammett.

This is a soap opera inspired episodic novel written specifically to continue similarly formatted themes from beloved daytime soap operas as well as memorable prime-time soap classics—but with adult storylines added. Nevertheless *Games People Play* was specifically written to resemble a filmed YouTube web series and though it occasionally imitates traditional classic soap operas to a certain extent—it was written with the intention that it's playing to a visual audience and therefore will emulate a scripted format (without camera angle directions) rather than the usual storytelling methods displayed in popular full-length novels such as *Bourne Identity* by Robert Ludlum. It should also be noted that each episode of this serialized novel were written in a brief span of 6-12 days or less and therefore shouldn't be confused with being great literature. The primary goal of this novel series was simply to mimic episodes of modern-day soap operas or filmed web series dramas—by creating visual entertainment on a printed page—and not to create a literary masterpiece.

The present storyline in *Games People Play* takes place approximately around the same time the drama in *Ocean Landing* concluded. Several existing characters from the Soap Opera Inspired Story Collection Series are included in this novel as well in order to continue several previously unfinished storylines.

Gary Brin
Series Creator

In an effort to have an accurate portrayal of the dialogue used for the *Soap Opera Inspired Story Collection Series* people were anonymously observed in shopping malls, schools, places of employment, and on public streets in order to capture a definitive portrayal of how people of various ages and cultures interacted and talked to each other when they thought no one was listening. While some select dialogue was exaggerated for dramatic purposes when needed—the manner and tone of which people were observed speaking to each other in casual and private conversations is accurate. Exact wording was not copied verbatim for the most part, but the way certain types of topics and conversations are addressed by characters in this serialized series is based on actual situations that were observed over a period of several dozen years.

Prologue

1
New Orleans
Less Than a Week Ago

"Two centuries give or take."

The man peers at the object in his hand and smiles broadly as he turns to face his eager young assistant.

"It's been hidden in this moldy tomb since the end of the Civil War. Who would have thought to look in a tomb?"

He turns around and looks at the coffins lying inside the cobweb-covered windowless building. He sighs loudly.

"I think we should leave now."

The man turns to look at his assistant.

2

"Don't lose sight of either of them."

A man dressed in an expensive business suit walks back and forth in front of a window fronting the French Quarter in downtown New Orleans. He seems irritated and stops.

"They must have found it—damn them."

He clenches his fist angrily and sighs loudly.

"Of course—do you even have to ask me such inane questions? Follow them back to their hotel room and rub them both out. Leave no witnesses behind—I've waited too long to get my hands on that frigging statue. I want them both dead."

He laughs and turns away from the window.

"He had partners no doubt—I want them in the morgue as well. Dead men tell no tales—do what must be done."

He clenches his fist yet again.

"I'll expect results before nightfall."

He sighs loudly as he shuts off his cell phone.

"If only Calvin and Eldon had lived to see this day."

He rubs his chin several times.

3

The view from the binoculars is clear as fingers reach out to adjust the lenses. Two men sit in a car several yards away from the entrance of an abandoned estate and watch the front gates with an intensity reserved for accomplished spies. They look at each other briefly before the one sitting in the driver's seat puts the binoculars down and rubs his eyes. He rubs his eyes again.

"We'll follow them and see where they go."

The other man nods in agreement.

"What if the Levitov brothers show up?"

There is a slight pause.

"We'll deal with them if we have to."

"That'll put a bounty on our heads courtesy of Whitney."

The man sitting in the driver's seat shakes his head and sighs loudly. He looks at the entrance of the estate again.

4

The man and his assistant slowly close iron doors to the mausoleum and walk to their car a few feet away. They stop.

"Do you think anyone saw us earlier?"

Page 14

They notice the eerie silence around them. The older man sighs and looks at the bulge under his jacket. He smirks.

"Does it look like anyone was looking? I doubt if anyone has been here in years. Every stiff here is over a century old."

The younger man seems uneasy.

5

"We have orders to take them both out."

Standing behind one of the large mausoleums they watch as the two men drive away. They turn to look at each other.

"Whitney is a gem without a doubt."

They both laugh.

"That man has ice water in his veins."

Seconds later they get into their car parked across the street. One of them pulls out a cell phone and begins dialing.

"We've got to keep that freak happy."

They both shake their heads in agreement.

6

People are moving about as two men slowly walk into a hotel and disappear inside the cavernous lobby. A few steps behind two men follow them—while behind them another man pulls out a cell phone and begins talking feverishly. He seems nervous as he begins speaking in Russian to someone on the other end. His behavior seems erratic and worsens as the seconds tick by. He clenches his fist several times and shrugs.

Page 15

A Brief Look at the First Episode

A search for a mysterious object sets several events into motion in multiple cities where murder is not a problem and greed makes for curious friendships among a team of dangerous rivals.

Look Back in Fear

1
San Francisco
Present Day

Lincoln Ross seems worried as he glances at his watch again and then at the vast terminal in front of him. He sighs loudly as people are milling around him from every direction.

"I bet he got lost—even though I told him."

He hears a laugh and turns around.

"I stopped to grab a bite."

Lincoln rolls his eyes knowingly and reaches out to hug his cousin. They look at each other briefly. Parker Ross glances at where David Sherwood is standing. He points and grins.

"This is my best friend David Sherwood."

Lincoln and David shake hands.

"Quite amazing both of you got into Point College."

Parker makes a gesture with his hand.

"We tweaked a few rules."

Lincoln lazily points his finger at his cousin.

"Uh-huh—I'll just bet you did."

He jabs Parker lightly.

"Your East Coast snooty behavior is annoying."

"Not my fault your dad decided to move to California after he graduated from San Francisco State back in the day."

Lincoln jabs Parker again.

"He saw opportunity—made a killing in Napa."

David notices a few women walking by and grins broadly.

"How are the women out here with dating?"

Lincoln shoots David a sly look.

"They're quite open to new ideas and positions."

Parker looks at David.

"David was quite popular in Castle Beach."

David winks.

"Chicks dig me—deal with it."

Lincoln turns to look at the exit.

"Guess we should head over to our new pad."

Parker grabs Lincoln's arm.

"You rented a house?"

Lincoln nods.

2

Lorraine McCall turns away from an antique mirror and seems upset as she looks at a strange object on a table nearby. The small statue-looking sculpture appears very, very old. She reaches out to pick it up cautiously and sighs loudly. She slowly slides her finger over the detailed grooves along the side. As her fingers slide toward the bottom, a feeling of terror suddenly overcomes her and she places the statue back on the table.

"Uncle Gerald really loved creepy things."

She glances at the rest of the objects scattered throughout the room. She shakes her head and walks toward a window a few feet away. She looks out. From behind her she feels a presence and turns around to see her older half-sister.

"I'm headed out to the mall—want to come?"

"How about we stop at Dairy Queen on the way?"

Evelyn Hayes nods and follows Lorraine out the door. As she leaves and closes the door behind her, the statue falls to the floor and rolls under a huge oak dresser a few feet away.

3

Stanley Ross shakes his head again as he looks at the paperwork in front of him. He seems upset as he faces the window of his office looking out toward Alcatraz Island.

"How could this happen?"

He slams his fist down on his desk.

"I was so careful."

He glances at the report in front of him.

"Goodbye Hillcrest Winery."

He leans back in his chair.

"At least I still have Marigold Publishing to rely on for the moment. Well, that and Gold Flower Creations in Berkeley."

He grabs his cell phone and dials.

4
Washington DC

"I told you already things aren't what they seem."

John Berringer sighs loudly as he walks back and forth in a covered parking lot. He stops and nods quickly several times.

"Of course I realize the implication of what happened with Gerald McCall. His death was certainly not by natural causes."

He grimaces and shrugs.

"I'm aware of what happened to him."

He glances at his car parked a few feet away.

"The question is what do we do now?"

He gestures with his hand.

"He seemed fine a week ago."

Loud yells can be heard coming from the cell phone.

"He royally pissed off someone no doubt."

He angrily clenches his fist.

"Fine—whatever you say—it's your skin not mine."

He shuts his cell phone off and sighs.

"What exactly did McCall find in New Orleans?"

Seconds later his cell phone begins buzzing as multiple messages begin appearing. He runs his fingers through his hair and clicks on the first one. An image of a plantation appears.

5
San Diego

"I thought you said we'd spend the afternoon together?"

Christian Malinger turns to look at his much younger girlfriend while pulling on a pair of boxer briefs. He shrugs.

"Got a call—got to go."

Marisa Sanz seems annoyed.

"I took off work for you."

Christian rolls his eyes and pulls on his Levi's.

"I'm sorry."

He pulls on a T-shirt and walks over to the bed with a smirk. They look at each other briefly before he leans over and kisses Marisa lightly on the lips. She kisses him back as he pulls away. He turns around and stops. He faces her and laughs.

"How about I come back tonight?"

Marisa rolls her eyes.

"You're just lucky you're hot."

"Hot and good in bed—don't forget that part."

He blows her a kiss and leaves seconds later. She leans back in bed and looks at the fresh stains on the satin sheets.

6

"What's the big deal about Gerald McCall?"

Tyler Fields turns to face Hugh Blandwick a few feet away.

"Why exactly is Orlov so determined to get his hands on the info McCall had? Dude was a liar—lied endlessly."

Hugh pulls out a handgun and hands it to Tyler.

"I don't know the gory details and really don't care."
Tyler slides his fingers across the barrel.
"I'm tired of being Orlov's lapdog. I want out."
They look at each other.

7
New Orleans

Cole Bouvier glances at the open door of the centuries-old mausoleum and shrugs. He turns to face William La Porte.
"Were the coffins disturbed?"
William shakes his head and sighs loudly.
"I have no idea."
He wipes sweat from his brow.
"I was told the door had been breached—that's all."
He faces the above-ground tombs once again.
"I haven't been here in years."
He sighs loudly again.
"It's been shuttered for almost a century at least. The rest of my relatives are buried elsewhere—mostly in town I think."
Cole pulls the door of the mausoleum shut.
"I'll have someone come by to inspect the coffins."
He leans toward William.
"Is there any possible reason why someone might want to disturb the final resting place of your distant relatives?"
William shakes his head and shrugs.

8

Tiffany Dennington smiles as she places a CD into a player and turns around to face a teenage boy. Marko Prinze grins.
"I brought plenty of condoms with me."
Tiffany rolls her eyes.
"I never said I would give myself to you."
He grins broadly.
"You didn't—but you will."

He makes a lewd gesture with his finger.

"I've got a sweet rep."

Tiffany sits down next to Marko.

"My dad hates you."

Marko laughs.

"That's even more of a reason to lose your virginity today—it'll really piss him off to know you gave it up to me."

Tiffany reaches out and strokes Marko's hand.

"My sister is still upset she lost her virginity to you on prom night—said you used her and then threw her away."

Marko smirks.

"I did no such thing. She was mad at Thad and took me up on my offer to fuck in the backseat of her car—end of story."

He begins to unzip his jeans.

"I didn't know she was still a virgin until I was already inside her and she blurted it out. I thought she and Thad Wreene had already slept together. Thad has a terrible rep with girls."

Tiffany watches Marko curiously as he gently takes her hand—seconds later her fingers slide over his stiff erection straining against his boxer briefs. He winks at her and sighs.

"Your father will be really angry when he finds out I took the virginities of both his daughters—he'll probably forbid you to see me after the fact—telling you how to live your life according to his fucked-up rules—and calling me **Brandon deWilde**."

Tiffany leans over to kiss Marko.

"I never listen to what my father says."

Marko kisses Tiffany passionately.

"How about we move this situation to my bed?"

Tiffany looks toward the door.

"What about your mother?"

Marko winks slyly and walks to the door. He locks it.

"My mother is no longer an issue."

Tiffany's eyes fall on his swelling erection.

"What if the condom breaks?"

Marko smirks as he extends his hand to Tiffany.

"I'll take you to an abortion clinic."

Tiffany seems confused.

"Has this happened to you already?"

Marko snickers.

"Uh-huh—it was no big deal."

Tiffany stands up.

9

"This isn't going to be easy."

Steve Andersen looks at a few sheets of paper spread out in front of him. He faces Erik Smith with a worried look.

"Tell me something I don't know."

Erik grabs several pieces of paper from Steve.

"Are you in or out?"

Steve stands up and looks at his watch nervously.

"What if we get caught?"

Erik rolls his eyes.

"Did we get caught in New Orleans?"

Steve sighs loudly.

"What if we're wrong about this place too?"

Erik seems annoyed.

"McCall had a fucking fortune with him when he dropped dead—like sixty-five frigging million dollars to be exact."

Erik shrugs as Steve sighs once more.

"Gerald McCall's family has no clue about the stuff he hid—they think he was a bumbling idiot—an oddball weirdo."

Erik looks at the pieces of paper in his hand.

"My great-great grandfather was the grandson of **Henry Morgan** and he told my grandfather before he kicked it he had a stash of gold coins—then died—took his secret to the grave."

Steve rolls his eyes and yawns loudly.

"Yeah yeah—and you think Gerald McCall found Morgan's loot. Stole it and hid it somewhere for safekeeping before he croaked—except there's no proof to that belief one way or the other. For the record this story is really beginning to reek like something lifted right out of some bad 1940s B movie."

Page 23

Steve snatches the pieces of paper from Erik.

"New Orleans was a dead end—nothing was inside the mausoleum we broke into—except a bunch of old coffins."

Erik grins slyly and waves his hand.

"Uh-huh—but who knew they buried people with jewelry back in the 1860s—made a killing selling what we found to a shady art dealer yesterday—that loser was seriously happy."

Steve looks at Erik curiously.

"Exactly what do you want me to do?"

Erik grins broadly.

10

Veronica Ross sighs loudly as her lawyer leans back in his chair with a worried look. Chad Winchester watches Veronica nervously as she glances at the paperwork in front of her.

"You can always change your mind?"

Veronica shakes her head.

"It's time I took action."

They look at each other for a few seconds.

"Stanley and I have been heading in this direction for years now—this won't be a shock to him. He expects it."

Chad taps his finger on top of his desk.

"Does he?"

Veronica nods.

"We've been estranged for two months."

Chad gives her a knowing look.

"What about the children?"

Veronica glances at the window briefly.

"Lincoln already knows and Roosevelt will adjust."

Chad stands up and walks to the window.

"Regardless I think you should take a day or two to think about what you really want to do. Come back when you do."

Veronica watches as Chad's gaze seems focused on the expanse of the Golden Gate Bridge in the far distance. She grabs the paperwork and heads to the door. She stops suddenly.

"Stanley doesn't suspect that you and I had an affair last year. As far as he's concerned you and I are just acquaintances and nothing more. He's not going to come after you in case you were wondering. He's not a revenge mongrel by any means."

Chad turns to face Veronica slightly upset.

"It never crossed my mind."

Veronica nods and reaches for the doorknob.

"Say hi to your wife."

Chad watches as Veronica leaves.

11

New Orleans

"La Porte was as clueless as we were on this case."

Wesley Trudeau shakes his head.

"Where does this leave us?"

Cole shrugs.

"Get the mausoleum inspected ASAP."

Wesley winces.

"Who's gonna be the lucky guy to inspect the stiffs?"

Cole glances at his cell phone and grins.

"Brian Delgado."

Wesley laughs loudly.

"He's gonna hate you for sure."

Cole grins slyly.

"He'll get over it."

He glances at the door nervously.

"It's time for him to face his fear of decaying bodies."

He sits down at his desk.

"He's much too freaky about old cemeteries—time he addressed that sooner than later. Besides, it's not my fault he likes binge-watching zombie movies on cable—serves young Delgado right if truth be told—such terrible acting. *Ugh*."

Wesley looks at the front door.

"He's due to start his shift any minute now."

Cole stifles a smirk and laughs.

Page 25

"I know. He certainly won't like what's coming."
They begin laughing in a mocking way.

12

"That view is something else."
David faces Lincoln as he turns away from the window overlooking San Francisco Bay. He gestures with his hand.
"How did you get this place so cheap?"
Lincoln looks at Parker.
"My dad leased it from one of his associates."
David and Parker share a look.
"Exactly how filthy rich is your dad?"
Lincoln looks at David curiously and rolls his eyes.
"He's got some dough."
David looks at the window again.
"It must be sweet to be rich."
Lincoln shakes his head.
"It has its moments."
David suddenly seems bored and sighs loudly.
"Is Alcatraz still in play?"
Lincoln nods.
"I booked tickets for next week."
Parker seems disappointed and shrugs.
"No sooner?"
Lincoln shakes his head.
"Place is usually booked solid months in advance."
Parker rolls his eyes.
"That sucks."
Lincoln glances at David and Parker with a curious stare as he pulls out a rolled-up newspaper from his jacket pocket.
"When were you going to tell me what really happened in Castle Beach last month? People are still talking about it."
David and Parker turn to look at each other nervously.
"Not much to tell. There was an outbreak of some weird tropical disease but the CDC got it under control quickly."

Page 26

Lincoln looks at Parker curiously.

"That's not the story you told me initially."

Lincoln looks at the newspaper again.

"As I recall you told me someone was stealing dead bodies from the morgue—and using them for nefarious reasons."

Parker glances at David.

"I know what I said—but I was wrong—that weird bug I told you about did things to the bodies—but the CDC was able to stop it from spreading—nothing more to tell—end of story."

Lincoln looks at Parker suspiciously.

"I don't buy it."

He glances at the newspaper again and sighs.

"According to the *Boston Herald* the CDC was never able to determine what really occurred—only that whatever was happening suddenly stopped as quickly as it had begun."

David walks over to Lincoln.

"It was seriously scary seeing people really sick—knowing they were going to die—not a pretty sight for anyone to witness firsthand if truth be known. Is that what you want to hear?"

Lincoln shrugs and turns away.

"I just thought the body snatching angle was wicked cool—like they did back in England in the eighteenth century."

David and Parker share a glance.

"This was nowhere as morbid as that."

He runs his fingers through his hair.

"It was a really scary nightmare in the daylight."

David sighs loudly and looks at Parker.

"Parker and I lost a lot of friends—really good friends. It all happened so fast—no warning. There were plenty of tears."

David faces Lincoln again.

"Not anything you'd want to experience."

He seems upset.

"How about we never talk about this again?"

Lincoln faces Parker.

"I can't make such promises."

David shoots Lincoln a strange look.

Marko winks as he pulls out of Tiffany. She watches as he stretches out in bed and sighs loudly. She reaches over to touch his hand. He looks at her and grins broadly. He sighs again.

"Are you going to miss being a boring virgin?"

Tiffany rolls her eyes.

"I'm not sorry about giving myself to you. I wanted you to be my first—to take me exactly the way you did my sister."

Marko laughs.

"Good call on your part I assure you."

Tiffany leans over to kiss Marko.

14
New Orleans

"I could swear that car was here yesterday."

William glances at a black sedan parked by the sidewalk in front of his home. He pulls into the driveway and turns to face the sidewalk again. The sedan suddenly drives away as he steps out of his car. He hears a noise behind him and as he turns—a strong muscular arm slides around his neck. William gasps for air.

"You have something I want."

William struggles as the grip around his neck tightens.

"Have what?"

His neck is jerked backwards.

"Keep it up—keep playing dumb—you'll regret it."

Without warning his assailant punches William in the chest with his other free arm. William reacts from the blow.

"You have one week to play ball."

Anton Levitov laughs.

"Then I kill you."

He throws William toward the pavement.

"One week."

William rubs his neck.

"Who are you?"
Anton viciously kicks William in the face twice.
"One week."
He turns to leave.
"If you talk to the cops I'll know."
He makes a slashing gesture with his finger across his neck as he slowly walks across the street toward a motorcycle.

15

Erik seems worried as he shuts off his cell phone and turns to look at Steve. His eyes fall on a map in front of him.
"There's an unfortunate snag in our plans."
He seems nervous and sighs.
"That was Rafael—word on the street seems to be that some operatives working for the Russian mob are on the trail of McCall's loot. It looks like some of our contacts are less than honorable when it comes to honesty—two-timers actually."
Steve rolls his eyes.
"What does that mean for us?"
Erik looks at the map again.
"It means we have to stay one step ahead of those Russian thugs—from what I've heard they are a pretty ruthless bunch."
He sighs loudly.
"Corpses left everywhere."
Steve watches as Erik stands up.
"Four people last night in the French Quarter in New Orleans—seven people last week in San Diego—and three more bodies found floating in Morro Bay about a week before that."
"Maybe they drowned?"
Erik seems about to laugh as he faces Steve.
"Yeah—except for the fact that they each had two huge bullet holes in their skulls—from Russian-made bullets."
Steve sighs loudly.
"This isn't fun anymore."
Erik's cell phone begins ringing.

Page 29

"Is it really over between you and dad?"

Veronica nods as she looks at the reaction of her teenage son. Roosevelt Ross glances at the tennis racket in his hand.

"Where am I going to live?"

Veronica shrugs.

"It's up to you."

Roosevelt looks up at the mansion a few yards away.

"I don't want to live in a studio apartment."

Veronica seems about to laugh.

"I rented a condo."

Roosevelt looks at the mansion again.

"Let me think about it."

Veronica nods.

17
San Diego

"This is quite disturbing."

Christian nods as he looks at Jared Goulet.

"Is there anything your brother might have been involved with that led to his death this morning? Like drugs? Or sex?"

Jared glances at Christian with a shocked look as he slowly leans back in his chair. He shakes his head several times.

"My brother was into art relics. He didn't do drugs and most certainly wouldn't be involved in the illicit sex trade."

Christian leans forward.

"You brother's body was found with Russian-made bullets lodged in his brain. He was most likely killed by someone working for the Russian mob. These are not nice people. They play dirty and kill their targets without even so much as a thought."

"Should I be worried for my safety?"

Christian points at Jared.

"Those guys don't have issues with murder."

Christian looks at the photos in front of him of seven bloated corpses. He reaches for his cell phone and sighs.

"Murder is a means to an end for them."

He sighs again.

"I recommend twenty-four-seven police protection."

Jared rolls his eyes and seems disgusted.

"I teach history at San Diego High. How is this going to look if I show up with a bodyguard? It'll be a freak show."

Christian stands up and walks over to Jared.

"Better a freak show than dead."

They look at each other.

"You said there were two other deaths yesterday? What was their connection to my brother and the other victims?"

Jared wipes sweat from his brow.

"Was one of them named Scott Bington?"

Christian looks at Jared curiously.

"Scott Bington?"

Jared wrings his hands several times.

"Bington is—was my brother's most recent assistant in hunting relics—he attends the University of San Diego."

Jared watches as Christian jots down Scott Bington's name. He glances back at the photographs on his desk.

"One of the victims was Dane McMarker. He was found about a mile away from where we found your brother's body. He was killed with Russian-made bullets also. From what I know he was a part-time courier of expensive statues for museums."

Jared looks at Christian angrily.

"My brother wasn't involved with art theft."

"I never said he was. But he was connected somehow to the victims in some way or the other is my best guess. Possibly through casual online associates—one of which was apparently McMarker. My guess is your brother was in the wrong place at the wrong time and was assumed to have info that someone clearly thought was worth killing for—and will kill again as long as whatever has become the object of interest remains elusive."

Jared reacts and sighs loudly.

18

Stanley shuts the door to his car and walks toward the back entrance of his mansion. He notices Roosevelt sitting in a pavilion at the edge of a garden and walks over to where his youngest son is sitting. Roosevelt looks up. He seems sad.

"What's up?"

Roosevelt watches as his father sits next to him. They stare at each other for a few seconds without saying a word.

"Having girl trouble at school?"

Roosevelt rolls his eyes.

"Been there—done that. Got dumped last month by Tammy Barnes—said I spent too much time playing tennis."

Stanley gestures with his hand and sighs.

"Isn't her father Riley Barnes?"

Stanley looks at his son.

"CEO of Barnes Electronics in Marin County—maker of those stupid puzzle boxes everyone thinks is a sweet deal."

Roosevelt nods.

"Uh-huh—but Tammy isn't the reason I'm in a funk."

Stanley seems confused.

"It's you and mom."

"What are you talking about?"

Roosevelt glances at the mansion.

"Talk to mom."

Stanley stands up.

19

"I can't be pregnant."

Sherry Barnes looks at herself in the mirror.

"It happened only one time. Marko promised me it couldn't happen the first time—he said he only shot blanks."

"And you believed him?"

Sherry turns around to look at her sister.

"He promised."

Tammy Barnes laughs.

"This is Marko Prinze we're talking about. He has a rep for a reason. He's slept his way through every girl at school. Rumor has it that he's also dallied with some of our teachers. Have you forgotten how fast our English teacher left last year? Word on the street was that she left because she got pregnant by one of the guys at school—want to guess who the proud papa could be?"

Sherry glances at her stomach.

"What should I do?"

Tammy rolls her eyes.

"Time for us to pay a visit to one of those public clinics on Haight-Ashbury and get you fixed before anyone finds out."

Sherry seems upset at the thought and sighs.

"Marko needs to know."

Tammy grabs Sherry by the arm.

20
Miami

Todd Whitney seems annoyed as he leans back in his chair. He glances at the cell phone on his desk and smirks.

"McMarker played a dangerous game."

He gestures with his hand.

"But Vladimir Orlov is not to be made a fool of. That worm McMarker deserved what Orlov did to him. Good riddance."

He laughs loudly.

"Let that be a lesson to non-believers."

As he turns to look at the Miami skyline he hears the door to his office open. He turns around to see Adam Sanchez holding a thick folder in his hand. He nervously takes a step forward.

"This is the info you asked for about that situation from Atlanta concerning Eldon's ex-wife. It's ready when you see fit to act. Corinne Rodson can be dealt with harshly if necessary."

Todd sighs loudly and nods.

"Thank you Adam. I appreciate your diligence."

Page 33

Adam nods and hands the folder to Todd and leaves. As he closes the door Todd looks at the folder. He thumbs through the paperwork and smiles broadly. He snaps his fingers twice.

"It's time I make Corinne see the light."

He clenches his fists.

"But I've got to figure out a plan of action—in case her lawyers get in the way. Of course there's always Plan B."

He grins slyly as he looks at a photo of Corinne Rodson and clenches his fists again. He closes the folder suddenly.

"She's trying my last nerve without a doubt."

He smirks and leans forward.

"Her demise would be justifiable after what she did."

He clenches his fist again and shrugs.

"Accidents happen every day in hazardous workplaces across this country—and what's more hazardous than a hospital emergency room where people with mental issues target those who try to help them—definitely something to think about."

He stands up and walks to the window.

21

"I think we can sell most of Gerald's crappy junk online."

Lorraine looks at Evelyn curiously.

"You really think so?"

Evelyn nods and takes a sip of coffee.

"People will buy anything. Better than just sitting on this junk for the next ten years—hoping it'll be worth something."

Lorraine sighs loudly.

"Gerald would freak royally if he could hear us right now talking about his collection as if it was just garage sale crap."

Evelyn rolls her eyes.

"Luckily he can't—he's dead."

She smirks.

"Life is for the living and that junk is garbage. This stuff might get us a few dollars if we're lucky—but nothing more."

Lorraine reacts and seems shocked.

"I forgot how mean you could be sometimes."
Evelyn grins broadly and gestures.
"I'm a realist—deal already."
She gestures with her hand again and laughs slyly.

22

"How about you and me see a movie later?"
Marko grins.
"I'll even see a chick flick."
Diane Singer looks at Marko curiously from behind the concession stand at the movie theater where she works.
"What about you and Tiffany Dennington?"
Marko cracks a smile.
"What about her?"
Diane looks at Marko suspiciously for a few seconds.
"I thought the two of you were a couple?"
Marko laughs.
"You thought wrong."
He makes a lewd gesture with his finger.
"I don't have a girlfriend."
He reaches out to stroke Diane's hand and winks.
"After the movie we can get to know the backseat of my car better—so many things we can do—it's been a long time."
Diane blushes.
"I missed you so much."
Marko tenderly kisses Diane's hand.
"I know—I missed you too."
He pulls her toward him and kisses her on the lips. She sighs loudly as he kisses her more passionately. As he pulls away from her she notices his erection straining under his Levi's.
"I'm on the pill—since two weeks ago."
Marko makes another lewd gesture with his finger as he kisses her again and looks down at his bulging erection.
"I like girls who come prepared."
He begins laughing.

Page **35**

New Orleans

"La Porte got the message loud and clear about what will happen to him. He knows the deal if he dares to cross me."

Anton laughs.

"This time next week there might be another corpse floating face down in one of those disgusting canals near the French Quarter if La Porte fails to take my threat seriously."

He grins broadly and laughs.

"What's one more corpse found in the canal? Place has more dead bodies than a morgue. Local gangs kill people every day for fun. Just today two guys were shot point-blank in front of a pansy barber shop. Heard the reason was simply because they were holding hands. I guess being openly gay can be deadly."

He makes a gesture with his hands and smirks.

"Oh well—maybe they should have been into girls."

He laughs loudly.

24

Stanley looks at Veronica and then glances at the folder in front of him. He wipes sweat from his brow and blinks.

"Is this really necessary?"

Veronica nods.

"It's for the best Stanley."

She turns around to look at the garden outside.

"I've already rented a condo on Nob Hill."

Stanley looks at Veronica.

"Isn't that a little pricy?"

Veronica sighs.

"It's my father's money in case you forgot."

Stanley grimaces.

"I only meant."

"I know what you meant."

Stanley looks at his watch for a second.

"I wish you wouldn't leave. But it's your choice."

He leaves the room.

"I guess I assumed it would be easy."

She turns around to see Roosevelt standing at the door.

25
San Diego

Christian looks at his watch and then at the house in front of him with a white picket fence and rose garden. He sighs.

"There's no pretty way to dress up murder."

He steps out of his car and walks toward the house.

26

Tyler tiptoes down the hallway as the floorboards creak under his feet. He looks around a few times and continues toward the room at the end of the hallway. Wind whistles through an open window creating swishing sounds. Tyler stops suddenly. As he turns to look toward the driveway below he notices Lorraine and Evelyn getting out of their car. He grits his teeth harshly.

"Fuck it. I thought they were gone for the day."

He looks back at the room at the end of the hallway.

"If they find me—death will find them."

Footsteps can be heard entering the house.

"Damn McCall for making this hard."

He darts into the room and hides behind a large stack of boxes. Seconds later he hears Lorraine and Evelyn coming up the stairs. He holds his breath as their footsteps seem to fade away a moment later. Silence permeates the room immediately.

27

"Does Lincoln know you've made it final with dad?"

Veronica looks at Roosevelt curiously.

"He does."
She glances at the front door.
"This is for the best."
Roosevelt watches as his mother walks past him toward the hallway leading upstairs. His cell phone begins to flash repeatedly with text messages from one of his classmates.

28

"You still haven't told me about this new guy you met last week at Miranda's bookstore? What's his name? Spill it."
Evelyn watches Lorraine's reaction to her question and gives her a knowing look. She turns away with a sly smile.
"There's nothing to tell."
Evelyn grabs Lorraine by the arm.
"From what Miranda said earlier the two of you were quite friendly. Flirted endlessly—teased each other nonstop."
Lorraine rolls her eyes.
"Remind me to cross Miranda Wu off my Christmas list."
Evelyn grins slyly.
"Don't blame Miranda for your behavior."
She glances at Lorraine's cell phone lying on a table a few feet away. Lorraine notices and quickly grabs the cell phone.
"I'm taking the fifth."
Evelyn tries to grab the cell phone.
"Miranda said he was some sort of artist?"
Lorraine smirks.
"Like I said I'm taking the fifth."
At that moment they hear creaking sounds upstairs. They look at each other for a few seconds. They seem alarmed.
"Is someone upstairs?"
Evelyn takes a step forward.
"Could be a homeless person?"
There is another loud creak and then silence.
"Think we should call the cops?"
Evelyn rolls her eyes.

Page **38**

"They'll take too long. Let's check it out."
Lorraine seems aghast at the idea.
"Maybe we should wait?"
Evelyn pulls out a small handgun from her purse.
"I've been taking lessons at the range."
Before Lorraine can answer Evelyn runs up the stairs and stops as she reaches the hallway. She cautiously takes a step forward and stops. Wind whistles through the hallway.
"Ugh. I really hate this house."
She turns to face Lorraine.
"How could Gerald live here all those years?"
They look at each other as the wind causes the floor to creak again. Evelyn laughs as she leans against the wall.
"This old house has a mind of its own."
They turn around and head downstairs again.

29

Tyler peeks through the bushes and then runs toward the street a few feet away. Hugh throws open the door to his car as Tyler climbs in seconds later. He's out of breath as he turns to look back at the house while Hugh seems upset and sighs.
"Did those two aging hens see you?"
Tyler shakes his head.
"This isn't going to be easy."
Tyler rolls his eyes.
"That place is full of junk."
He sighs loudly.
"McCall had bad taste—*like* really bad taste. But it has to be in that house somewhere—somewhere in all that junk."
Tyler looks back at the house.
"Those two women might be a problem."
He runs his fingers through his hair and sighs loudly.
"I might have to take them out permanently."
"Orlov won't care either way."
Hugh shakes his head several times.

"Those Russian mob types play for keeps."
Tyler wipes sweat from his brow.
"His freak show goons killed my brother last year. They tossed him into San Francisco Bay like a used piece of trash after they handcuffed him to a fifty pound piece of cinder block."
His expression changes as he turns to face Hugh.
"I'm done. This isn't worth it."
Hugh nervously looks back at the house.
"Orlov will kill you."
Tyler shrugs.
"He'll have to find me first."
Hugh's cell phone begins to ring loudly.
"What about me?"
Tyler looks at Hugh curiously.
"*Does everything always have to be about you?*"
Hugh angrily grabs Tyler by his shirt collar.
"I'm involved in this mess also in case you forgot."
Tyler pushes Hugh away.
"I'm tired of dealing with Orlov and his people."
Hugh laughs nervously.
"Don't forget Orlov is tight with San Francisco's finest."
He looks at his cell phone again.
"Most of the San Francisco PD works for the Russian mob and take their orders directly. You're a dead man walking."
Tyler wrings his hands.
"I want out."
Hugh shows Tyler his cell phone and sighs.
"Orlov is calling me directly. He's not happy with us."
Tyler looks away.

30

Vladimir Orlov slams his cell phone down on his desk.
"That jerk is trying my last nerve."
He faces Bruce Copeland.
"Find that ungrateful miserable wretch."

Page **40**

Bruce smirks knowingly.

"And when I do?"

Vladimir grins broadly.

"It's time for him to join his brother in San Francisco Bay."

He walks over to where Bruce is standing.

"Hire someone classy to film his bon voyage."

Bruce touches his badge as Vladimir hands him a gun wrapped in a rolled-up newspaper and makes a lewd gesture.

"Shoot him in the knee but don't kill him."

He laughs slyly.

"I want him to know what's happening when he's thrown from the Golden Gate Bridge by you and Erwin. His death will be a warning to anyone else stupid enough to defy me. I will not tolerate useless garbage like that wretch disrespecting me by refusing to follow my orders. Take him out at midnight."

Bruce nods and leaves Vladimir's office.

TO BE CONTINUED

A Brief Look at the Second Episode

Desperation leads to plenty of mistakes for several people as errors in judgment begin to create fissures among friends while a failed marriage finally comes to an end as a reporter reluctantly follows up on a story that seems to be leading nowhere.

Ties That Bind

1
New York City

"Tell me again why this is a story?"

Scott Malone watches as Roland Parker leans back in his chair. He smirks as he flips a pencil in the air. Scott shrugs.

"I already did—*twice*. Word on the street is that Stanley Ross is involved with some shady dealings—and art theft."

Scott rolls his eyes.

"This sounds really boring."

Roland seems annoyed.

"Frigging art theft is serious business with the jet set Malone. They take that stuff seriously—those silver spoons places more value on a piece of canvas than they do human life."

Scott looks at his watch.

"Fine whatever—when do I head out to the coast?"

Roland grins broadly.

"Four hours—booked you first class on American Airlines just before you got here. Tell Sandra goodbye and scram."

Scott waves his hand in the air and sighs.

"She won't like this deal one bit."
Roland shrugs.
"Tell me something I don't already know."
Scott looks at his watch again.

2

Tyler Fields shuts off his cell phone and faces Hugh Blandwick. He seems upset as he glances across the street.
"I'm a dead man."
Hugh smirks.
"I told you as such."
Tyler wipes sweat from his brow.
"I've got to make tracks fast."
He looks at his cell phone again and sighs.
"I think it's time I make good with my ex while I figure things out. She still has feelings for me—despite what happened between me and her sister—she seemed open to getting back together the last time we talked—got to play the idea out."
Hugh watches as Tyler begins dialing.

3

Lincoln Ross turns around to look at David Sherwood and Parker Ross. They notice the worried expression on his face.
"It's official—my parents are splitsville."
Parker reacts.
"How did your father take it?"
Lincoln shrugs and glances at David.
"I'm not sure exactly. He seemed in denial."
Parker walks over to where Lincoln is standing.
"Maybe they'll patch it up?"
Lincoln shrugs.
"Doubt it—too much drama to ignore."
David's cell phone begins ringing. He looks at it and sighs loudly. He seems visibly upset as he faces Parker and Lincoln.

Page **44**

"It's Cassandra."
Parker gestures with his hand.
"Didn't you end it with her last week?"
David points at Parker.
"I did—thought I made it clear to her—stated it was nice while it lasted but I'd moved on—decided to see other girls."
Lincoln winks at David.
"What if she pays you a visit?"
David shakes his fist at Lincoln.
"Don't even say something like that out loud—Cassie is no wallflower by any means. She knows I'm here in Frisco."
He runs his fingers through his hair.
"I met her at a press conference CNN held in Boston right after—right after that CDC story broke—she thought we had something going—but we were just friends—nothing more."
Parker jabs David.
"Did you tell her that before you slept with her?"
David grins slyly.
"Didn't think it mattered."
Lincoln makes a lewd gesture with his finger and grins.
"Maybe she's pregnant?"
David shoots Lincoln a cautious look.

4
London

Dirk Hawkins looks at the computer screen in front of him as he watches an image begin to come into focus—seconds later he watches Pierce Colby on a monitor staring back at him from Boston. Dirk looks at several folders in Pierce's hand.
"This is happening as we speak?"
Pierce nods.
"Uh-huh—I was alerted just minutes ago by the FBI."
Dirk leans back in his chair and sighs loudly.
"I guess anything is certainly possible."
He glances at a painting of a young man on the wall.

"My great-great-great-great grandfather was quite the rebel in his youth—his adventures in the Caribbean as a cabin boy among a band of pirates thrilled each and every one of his descendants. But I never took it seriously—seemed more like he made up a tall tale when he returned from his voyage."

He runs his fingers through his hair.

"He left a detailed diary of his experiences that was passed down through my family but I've never read it."

Pierce reacts.

"No one attempts to break into a locked vault unless they are looking for something specific. That old diary must have info someone wanted badly—especially with the efforts made."

Dirk seems bothered by the statement.

"My father gave the diary to the Smithsonian when I was away at college. He was tight with someone there and gladly handed it over when asked. That was sixteen years ago."

They look at each other.

"What happens now?"

Pierce shrugs.

"I'm expecting a call anytime from my friend at the FBI. He said they're watching surveillance video by the truckloads."

"What about the diary? Where is it now?"

Pierce gestures with his hand.

"Still locked away in the manuscript section—no one is going to get their hands on it now—security has been tripled."

Pierce's cell phone begins to buzz.

"That's my friend now—I'll check back as soon as I speak with him—this could be the beginning of something big."

Dirk nods as he watches the monitor go blank.

"Who'd think after all these years a lame story about buried treasure in the Caribbean could actually be true?"

He begins to laugh as he leans back in his chair again.

"If only my father had known?"

He smiles broadly and glances at his cell phone.

"Buried treasure on some godforsaken island in the British West Indies hidden by a band of marauding cutthroats."

He grabs his cell phone and stops suddenly.

"I think it's time I talk with an expert."

He begins dialing. Seconds tick by as he waits nervously rubbing his hands. He sighs as the line is finally picked up.

5
New York City

"I know I promised we'd spend this coming weekend at Cape Cod. But you know how crazy Roland can be when he thinks there's a hot story brewing. He's fit to be tied no doubt."

Scott watches as Sandra King wags her finger.

"I swear I'm going to hurt that man one of these days."

Scott grins broadly.

"Make sure I have a front row seat."

He pulls Sandra toward him and hugs her warmly.

"I'll miss you."

Sandra kisses Scott.

"One week."

Scott nods.

"I promise."

They embrace for a few minutes.

6

Lorraine McCall sighs loudly as she glances at the paperwork in front of her and then at the realtor standing next to her with several folders in his hand. Travis Sweeney shakes his head as he notices Lorraine's apparent misgivings about signing a document giving control of the property to his company.

"This is the best way to unload an old house that will have to be remodeled in order to make it viable for new tenants."

"I know—it's just that I thought I had more time."

Travis shakes his head.

"I have an interested party already."

Lorraine sighs loudly.

Page **47**

Boston

Maxwell Pendergraft shakes hands with Pierce and grins as he watches Pierce close the door to his office. They walk toward the desk at the far end of the office. Maxwell sighs.

"Like I told you earlier, we found video footage of the attempted robbery at the Smithsonian. The potential thief was professional without a doubt—seemed to know all the right moves to make—except for the last sensory device."

"What would someone possibly want with an ancient diary from the eighteenth century written by an adventurous obscure teenage boy detailing his voyage to the British West Indies?"

Maxwell shrugs.

"I'm clueless on that front—but our clever thief went to a lot of trouble to get his hands on this particular manuscript."

He waves his hands in the air.

"An electronic copy is being made from the original as we speak—there's obviously something within its pages worth stealing—possibly something to do with what your client from London said was a tall tale perpetrated by the writer of the diary—who happens to be his grandpa four times removed. I assume you've made Dirk Hawkins aware of the latest?"

Pierce nods.

"I have."

Maxwell looks out the window at the Boston skyline.

"It's good to be back in Boston—been traveling back and forth to the West Coast regularly since my college buddy and his wife moved out there—said they wanted a fresh start."

He grins slyly.

"They bought a house in Pasadena—said the weather is always perfect year round—so I visited—and stayed—and stayed longer. They just had a baby. But I miss the changing of the seasons though—especially summer and fall—like I said, it's good to be back on the East Coast after a spell—feels like home."

Pierce shakes his head.

"How's your father?"

Maxwell suddenly becomes tense.

"He's doing fine—it took a while but he finally feels like his old self again. No thanks to that punk kid that hit him."

Pierce leans back in his chair.

"I know it was a good idea to send you to Jeremy Winterfield after you told me what happened. I never had any doubt he would right the wrong that was done to your pop."

Maxwell stifles a smirk.

"Jeremy Winterfield is a badass without a doubt. I heard Carson Penney had a heart attack after he was served with papers from Winterfield. It must have been quite a shock for Penney to lose his son and then less than twenty-four hours later find out the lawsuit against his late son was still going ahead."

Pierce leans forward.

"Jeremy is no shrinking violet. After Carson Penney died he upped the ante and forced the surviving Penney children to settle out of court—of which led to the dissolution of most of Penney's ill-gotten money. His company closed within weeks and the remaining assets were sold cheap to the highest bidder."

Maxwell rolls his eyes.

"I wish I could feel some sort of pity for Carson Penney but he was a troll—a rotten excuse for a human being who got exactly what he deserved. With any luck his remaining children will turn out differently now that they've been dealt a dose of reality."

He wrings his hands.

"That reminds me—what's the deal with Howard—I mean the Blake Madison case—was there any truth to the stories."

Pierce stands up and stretches.

"There's still idle chatter in Marble Hills that maybe something nefarious happened at Glass Owl that afternoon."

Maxwell waves his hand in the air.

"The story we got from eyewitnesses matched everything the coroner said after he performed an autopsy on that wretched old man. His family seems disinterested in any further probes."

Page 49

He watches Pierce's reaction.

"Case was closed over a year ago—there was no interest to pursue any further investigations. I was reassigned soon after to New York and then to Los Angeles. From where I stand Blake Madison and Carson Penney were cut from the same cloth."

He sighs loudly.

"I was quite pleased however to see his daughter use the money left to her to start a school for those less privileged."

Pierce smiles broadly.

"I'm so proud of Gina Bentley. Glass Owl was torn down and in its place is a campus that now has over twelve thousand students from around the United States and its territories."

He walks toward the window.

"She's turned her life around without a doubt—going from a troubled teenager to one of the most influential benefactors in North America and Europe—named the school after one of her classmates that her deranged half-sister viciously murdered."

Maxwell nods in agreement.

"I remember the case quite well. She was the reason I came to Marble Hills initially—then everything went haywire."

"There's a movie in the works about the murders."

Maxwell faces Pierce and shrugs.

8

"I already told you—he skipped."

Hugh runs his fingers through his hair and faces Vladimir Orlov once more. He seems nervous as he watches Vladimir's cold reaction. Behind him a muscular man in T-shirt and Levi's takes a step forward. Hugh looks at Vladimir again. He sighs.

"I warned him you'd be mad."

Vladimir leans forward and points to Hugh.

"You better hope that we find your worthless friend."

He pounds his fist on top of his desk.

"I paid both of you to take care of that problem McCall left behind. Paid you handsomely as I recall and I expected results."

Page **50**

Hugh nods and looks around once more as the muscular man seems only a few inches away from him. He shrugs.

"I know. I'll make it up to you. I promise."

Vladimir laughs.

"Oh, I know you will—because if you don't stick to your word—my brother Sergei will crush you like a bug. Break plenty of bones that will guarantee you never walk again—do I make myself clear Blandwick? I always keep my word—especially when it comes to making sure those who cross me learn a lesson."

Hugh turns to look at Sergei Orlov nervously. Sergei laughs and flexes his arms several times. Hugh sighs.

"I won't let you down again."

Vladimir makes a gesture to Sergei.

"See that you don't—Sergei is anxious to test his strength on your feeble body. He likes beating people up—likes putting people in wheelchairs for the rest of their lives—he's quite the charmer when he wants to be in case you were wondering—think about that when you go back to your studio apartment—knowing that I'm watching your every move from this day forward."

Hugh nods again and sighs loudly.

9

San Diego

"Is that all you have on this story at the moment?"

Christian Malinger seems annoyed as he glances at Harcourt Styverson sitting across from him in a greasy diner.

"No one's talking—word must be out."

Christian rolls his eyes.

"I spoke to Jared Goulet earlier. He knows nothing or so he says anyway. But there's something going on—Goulet seemed scared when I asked about his brother—seemed panicked."

"Think we should put several plain clothes on his trail for a few days to see if anything is happening behind the scenes?"

Christian nods several times.

"Uh-huh—I think that's a good idea."

Page **51**

Christian looks at his cell phone lying nearby and sighs.
"I have Kelker out looking for Scott Bington."
Harcourt shrugs.
"Do you think he's still among the living?"
Christian stands.
"No idea."
He nervously runs his fingers through his hair.

10

Oceanside

Scott Bington looks at himself in the mirror while he carefully empties a bottle of hair coloring over his blond hair as a few drops carelessly fall on the floor. He sighs loudly as he nervously looks at himself in the mirror. He looks at his watch and then at the mirror again. He wrings his hands several times.
"I hope this disguise works or I'm a dead man."
He sighs loudly and reaches out to touch his hair.

11

Parker watches as David sits in a folding chair on the patio and looks out at San Francisco Bay. He sighs loudly.
"This view beats Castle Beach."
Parker jabs David and sits down next to him.
"Have you spoken to your folks?"
"What do I look like to you—a baby?"
He laughs.
"I'll call them tomorrow."
He makes a lewd gesture with his finger and smirks.
"They've got their own lives to live."
He waves his finger in the air.
"They said as much when they found out I was headed west for college instead of going to Boston University like they assumed I would initially. I was quite a handful if you recall."
Parker jabs David again.

Page **52**

"Do you still think about what happened?"

David turns to face Parker.

"I try not to ever go there—best leave what happened in the past—not even the scariest horror movie can prepare you for real life. What happened to your cousin and the others is something I won't ever forget—terrible—really terrible."

Parker turns to look at the house.

"How do you like Lincoln?"

David turns to look where Parker's gaze is fixated.

"He seems OK—more self-assured than you in case it matters. Typical rich kid with too much money to spend."

Parker rolls his eyes.

"My cousin might be a bit much—but he's always going to have your back if you need it—steadfastly loyal to a fault."

David gestures with his hand.

"Good to know."

Parker leans forward.

"I've been thinking about contacting that writer we met back in Castle Beach—you know the one who wanted to write a book about what happened—said it would sell millions."

David reacts.

"Uh-huh—think about what you're saying Parker. Talking to a writer will open up a can of worms. How will you explain what took place at that creepy old cemetery—and what we did?"

Parker leans back in his chair.

"I see your point."

He sighs loudly.

"I guess I should lose his number. No use being tempted by the lure of millions when it could backfire royally."

David makes a lewd gesture with his finger again.

"You think?"

David looks back at the house.

"How are the folks handling you being away?"

"They still think I'm a child."

David and Parker share a knowing glance.

12

Scott glances at his watch as he steps out onto the balcony of his hotel room. He sighs as he listens to the voice on his cell phone. He seems amused for some reason and shrugs.

"Got it Roland—relax already. I booked an interview with Stanley Ross yesterday. I'm meeting him later for lunch."

Scott rolls his eyes.

"Enough already with the screaming—I've got it in the bag. I'll be back in a few days—get my bonus check ready."

He smirks.

"Yeah—yeah—I know what happens if I fuck up."

He walks back into his hotel room.

"Stanley Ross has no idea that his art gallery was bought by some mysterious outfit based in Miami—with mob ties."

He nods several times.

"Of course I plan to spring it on him when we meet—give me credit for knowing my job—his reaction will be telling."

He stops and sighs loudly.

"The bigger question I have for you—why would anyone give a damn about an art gallery that barely cleared a million last year? What's the big deal about lame sculptures anyway?"

Scott gestures with his hand.

"OK—OK—don't have a stroke."

He sits down on the sofa.

"As you say—your wish is my command."

Scott nods several more times.

13

Kevin Kulkovich looks at the sledgehammer in his hand and then turns to face Igor Levitov. He grins broadly.

"McCall's crypt is close to the entrance of the cemetery."

He runs his fingers through his hair.

"He probably thought he could take it with him."

He makes a lewd gesture with his finger.

"Tomorrow morning will certainly be quite the shock for the groundskeeper—finding McCall's rotting body outside his crypt will make for an entertaining morning no doubt."

Igor seems upset at the comment.

"Do you think it smells bad?"

Kevin shakes his head.

"He was laid to rest this morning—the embalming job he got will keep his body intact for several weeks give or take."

He sighs and makes a lewd gesture with his finger again.

"Bodies buried in crypts have to be embalmed."

Igor reacts.

"What about worms?"

Kevin seems annoyed and shrugs.

"Stop being a puss Igor."

He jabs Igor.

"You're definitely nothing like your brothers."

He rolls his eyes and jabs Igor again.

"Your mother must have really done a serious job on you when you were little—turned you into a world-class wimp."

Igor turns away seemingly upset.

"Leave my mother out of this—she's a saint."

Kevin winks slyly.

"Uh-huh—I'll just bet."

Kevin jabs Igor again and laughs.

"Where is your brother anyway?"

Igor shrugs.

"I'm not sure exactly—New Orleans I think."

He looks at his watch.

"He's been busy lately."

Kevin smirks.

"Orlov has him on a tight leash I bet."

Igor sighs loudly.

"I know the feeling."

He clenches his fist and seems bothered.

"No one says no to Vladimir Orlov—unless they want to end up in a ditch down the coast—Anton mentioned things that Orlov has done to people who dared go up against him."

He lowers his voice.

"Orlov's not playing with a full deck."

Kevin laughs loudly.

"What does that say about us?"

Igor seems confused.

14
San Diego

"I don't know anything—this is a mistake."

Jared Goulet watches as Anton Levitov circles him several times. He tries to back away and feels a gun pressed against his back as his younger brother Sasha Levitov laughs loudly.

"There's bullet with your name on it."

He grins broadly.

"Think before you act Goulet."

Jared seems panicked as he looks at Anton.

"I have no idea what you think I have."

He sighs.

"I don't know how many times I have to say it."

Sasha rams his fist into Jared's chest. Anton laughs.

"Until you mean it—until you give me what I want—what I'm owed—there's no way out for you—my brother enjoys hurting people and I know for a fact he wants to exercise his fists on your face. He needs a release every now and then—breaking a few bones in your body will do nicely—until he feels the need again to use you as a punching bag—this could last for several hours."

Anton walks over to Jared and winks at Sasha.

"I think we should make it clear to Goulet we're not fooling around with him—a broken arm should do the trick."

Sasha nods in agreement. Before Jared can react Sasha spins him around and twists his arm backwards until a snapping sound is heard. Jared screams as Anton begins laughing.

"I don't want you seeing Marko Prinze again."

Diane Singer shakes her head as she looks at her father standing a few feet away from her. He seems visibly upset.

"I don't care what you say daddy—I'm not going to stop seeing him. He likes me—and I like him—deal with it."

Eugene Singer walks over to where his daughter is sitting and sits down opposite her. He angrily grabs her hand.

"I'm not going to tell you twice."

Diane pulls her hand free.

"You can't tell me what to do."

Eugene lunges at his daughter in a rage.

"I can and I will."

He slaps her hard.

"If you defy me and pay young Mr. Prinze a visit I'll have to act—and it would be really terrible if something highly unpleasant happened to your friend. Heed my warning—I will make good on my threat—and you'll have no one else to blame but you."

Diane reacts as Eugene stands up.

"I know you had Alexander Woodley killed."

Eugene turns to face Diane.

"That's right I did—I said I would kill him if he dared to see you again—he did and I had him taken out. It's your fault he's occupying a plot on a hillside at Colma—you killed him."

Diane begins to cry.

"I hate you."

Eugene laughs and waves his hand in the air.

"You can't hate your father—I'm you—you're me."

Diane wipes a tear from her eye.

"If you hurt Marko I'll tell."

Eugene flies into a rage and grabs Diane by the arm. He spins her around and slaps her hard across the face. He hits her again several times as she screams. He finally lets her go.

"How dare you threaten me?"

He raises his hand again as she screams.

"Stay away from that punk."

He sighs loudly.

"I'm not going to tell you again."

He storms out of the room. Diane looks at herself in the mirror and reaches out to touch the welts on her face.

"I hate him."

She begins to cry.

"I really do."

Tears stream down her face.

16
New Orleans

"Where's Delgado?"

Wesley Trudeau turns to face Cole Bouvier and smirks as he slowly sits down at his desk. He points to the parking lot.

"He's on his way."

He laughs.

"He's still traumatized about the cemetery deal."

Cole grins broadly.

"Think we should make zombie jokes?"

Wesley gestures with his hand.

"I'm game if you are."

They both begin laughing as Brian Delgado enters. He notices and shoots them dirty looks. They laugh even harder.

"Nothing beats walking through a cemetery at five in the afternoon—just as the sun goes down and shadows begin dancing every which way you look—party central for spooks."

Brian makes a lewd gesture with his finger.

"Both of you are marked—just so you know—I'll get even when you least expect it—my grandmother knows things."

Cole stands up.

"I'm so scared Delgado."

He walks over to where Brian is standing and slaps him on the back. They pretend to shadowbox for several seconds.

"You have to admit it was funny sending you to that old cemetery—nothing worse than bodies over a century old."

He looks at Wesley knowingly.

"Think we should sign Delgado up for a shrink?"

Brian pushes Cole and sits down at his desk.

"Like I said I'll get even—count on it."

Cole and Wesley laugh.

"OK—fine—be that way Delgado—take it personally."

He walks back toward his desk and stops.

"Were any of the stiffs in the crypt disturbed?"

Brian shakes his head.

"Four of the ten coffins showed some signs of being breached. But the remains were much too decayed to know for sure if any personal belongings had been removed. I'm going to pay William La Porte a visit later today to update him."

Cole leans back in his chair.

"Good work Delgado. There's hope for you yet."

Brian ignores Cole and faces his computer.

17

Roosevelt Ross watches as his mother places several pieces of clothing into an oversized suitcase. He sighs loudly.

"I guess you're really leaving dad?"

Veronica Ross turns to face her youngest son.

"I wish there was another way."

She watches as he walks over to her.

"You can move in with me anytime you want—the condo has plenty of room—the view is great—just like a movie."

Roosevelt waves his hand in the air.

"I'm still thinking about it."

He walks toward the window and stops suddenly.

"I'm never getting married."

Veronica seems shocked at the comment.

"Why would you say that?"

Roosevelt shrugs.

Page **59**

"Everyone I know is from a broken home—and now you and dad are on the outs. Why bother getting married when it'll just end in a divorce—one that is drawn out and nasty."

Veronica looks at Roosevelt curiously.

"Just because your father and I couldn't make it work doesn't mean you and Lincoln will have the same fate."

Roosevelt rolls his eyes.

18

Oceanside

"We've got to make tracks—fast—before it's too late."

Scott nervously looks at his sister Carla Bington as they pull out of the motel driveway and head toward the highway.

"I told you that man would get us in trouble."

Scott glances at Carla.

"He didn't do anything wrong—he just found something other people wanted—and they killed him for it. That's all."

Carla rolls her eyes.

"What about that McCall jerk?"

Scott looks at the highway ahead before he faces Carla.

"I don't know anything about him or what he did to piss so many people off—but Goulet was legit all the way. He would never do anything shady—he was killed for no reason."

Carla wipes sweat from her brow.

"What do we do now?"

Scott shrugs and faces his sister again.

"I have no idea—we're winging it—I'll see."

He notices multiple cars following them on the highway as they enter the freeway up ahead. A few of the cars pass by but two seem to be keeping steady pace with them. He sighs.

"I think we have company."

Carla turns to look. She seems panicked.

"What should we do?"

Scott shrugs as he glances over his shoulder.

"Keep calm. Just keep calm for now."

They pass several police cars and slow down as they see a sign indicating Orange County is several miles away. They look at the rearview mirror again and notice the two cars are closer than before. Carla fearfully grabs Scott's arm. He shakes his head.

"If Orlov and his men are following us we have no chance whatsoever—they'll blow us away without hesitating."

Carla looks back again at the two cars.

"Are you sure you don't have something they want?"

Scott shoots Carla a strange look.

"I already told you I didn't."

Up ahead, Scott notices an off ramp and exits the San Diego Freeway. He turns into several side streets and seem to be lost among a neighborhood of track houses. He sighs.

"I think we gave them the slip."

Carla smiles weakly as she realizes there is no one behind them. Scott seems pleased as he turns into another street and comes upon a cul-de-sac. He tries to turn around and realizes one of the cars that were following earlier is right behind them.

"We're royally fucked."

Two men step out of the car.

19

Eugene looks back at his house as he walks out onto a small tree-shaded patio. He stops and pulls out his cell phone.

"That daughter of mine needs to learn a lesson about not trying my patience—that Prinze boy is on borrowed time."

He laughs as he continues dialing.

"A scare might be in play for that horny college punk."

He sighs as he looks back at the house again.

"One warning will be enough to teach that stupid jerk a lesson before he does anything else that would require me to decide on his fate—resulting in a trip to the local morgue."

He gestures with his finger.

"If he persists he'll end up at Colma rather quickly."

He begins laughing loudly with glee.

20
London

"I know what it looks like Reginald. Some bizarre old story told by my long-dead grandfather four times removed is suddenly on everybody's tongue. But it is what it is—plain and simple."

Reginald Balding seems confused.

"But I thought you said the stories told by Jim Hawkins about a bunch of pirates was just in his mind—and that it never happened—said he embellished his experiences as a lowly cabin boy to impress his children so he wouldn't seem so dull."

Dirk Hawkins shakes his head.

"Like I said—it all seemed bogus—but apparently it wasn't a tale after all—and with that said Reginald—I need your help."

They look at each other for a few minutes.

"I still don't understand."

Dirk looks at the cell phone in his hand.

21
Napa Valley

Bruce Copeland stands before Vladimir as he holds Tyler in front of him at gunpoint. Vladimir smiles broadly.

"Did you think I'd just let you skip town motherfucker?"

He looks around at an empty winery.

"Did you think I would allow it?"

He smirks and confidently walks toward Tyler.

"I think we know what this means for you."

Vladimir pulls out a hunting knife from his jacket. He grins broadly as he turns to look at Tyler. He watches Tyler's terrified reaction as he boldly takes a step closer. He laughs loudly.

"You brought this upon yourself."

He and Bruce exchange looks.

"No one crosses me and escapes my wrath."

Tyler seems panicked.

"Please—please don't. I'm sorry."

Vladimir waves the knife in the air and grins slyly.

"Trust me, you're going to know the meaning of sorry, you ungrateful wretch. Your slight simply can't go unpunished."

He looks around at the expanse of grape vines.

"I bet you don't know where you are right now. Bet you have no idea this is where they filmed that old series *Falcon Crest* decades ago. That show had it all—plenty of backstabbing, lying, murdering and cheating schemes galore. No one was ever happy no matter what they did. Nothing ever went as planned."

He looks at the knife in his hand.

"You shouldn't have crossed me Fields. It was a dumb move—one that will cost you your life. But hey, look on the bright side for a second—at least you don't have to run anymore."

He winks at Bruce.

"When I finish gutting you with this knife—Bruce and I will call the authorities and report your death—laugh about it."

He smirks and kisses the knife.

"But I—please—oh please—I'll do."

Less than a second later Vladimir rams the knife into Tyler's chest, slashing downward as blood gushes from the wound. Tyler cries out in shock. Bruce begins laughing as he watches Vladimir ram the knife into Tyler's chest again and again while blood spills out along with parts of his internal organs. As Vladimir rips open the wounds in Tyler's chest, he watches as the doomed man reacts in shock as he realizes what's happening.

"We all have to go sometime—deal already."

Vladimir continues hacking at Tyler's chest until the wound is a mangled mess. He laughs several times as he realizes Tyler is dead. He grabs Tyler's head and begins hacking at his neck until his head is lopped off. Vladimir holds it up proudly.

"This is *so* going to send a message."

He drops the head on the ground and wipes the blood from his hands on his faded Levi's. He looks around the area.

"You think he appreciated my insightful commentary on *Falcon Crest*? I got the distinct impression he didn't care much."

Bruce shrugs as they look at the gutted body lying a few feet away from them. Vladimir smirks and stifles a laugh.

"Hugh Blandwick better watch his step."

He looks at the knife in his hand.

"He could be next on the carving block."

Bruce looks at the knife and sighs.

"I think we should definitely kill him also—he's outlived his usefulness to us—it's just a matter of time before he blabs."

Vladimir begins laughing.

"I like the way you think Bruce—no wonder my father appreciated you—you've got plenty of spirit—and spite."

Bruce turns to face the abandoned winery.

"Your father was a hero to me."

Vladimir seems pleased.

22

Igor watches as Kevin drops two sledgehammers into the trunk of his car and turns around. He wipes sweat from his brow as he glances at the walled crypts several yards away.

"There was nothing with the stiff—McCall didn't take it with him as we assumed—or maybe someone helped themselves to whatever he had with him at the time he up and croaked."

He clenches his fist angrily.

"I think it's time we pay Lorraine McCall a visit. Broke a few bones in that dried up body of hers—send a message."

He stops and faces Igor again.

"Give or take a few days. Give her time to get over the shock of finding out her uncle's final resting place was opened and his body sloppily pulled out onto the hallway—by unknown individuals looking for what wasn't McCall's in the first place."

He opens the door to his car.

"The cops are going to be crawling all over this place within the next hour or so. But there'll be no clues—just a body lying outside a casket that has sledgehammer dings to it."

Igor begins laughing at the comment.

Page **64**

23

"How many times do I have to tell you—I have no idea what this Orlov person wanted with my teacher. I wasn't privy to any shady dealings if there were any. I have no reason to lie."

Harcourt looks at Scott and Carla. He sighs.

"Listen—someone thought nothing of murder in order to get their hands on whatever they were seeking. You two aren't safe as long as they're on the loose. They play for keeps."

Scott runs his hands through his hair.

"I just want to be normal again."

He shrugs.

"What are you gonna do to us?"

Harcourt seems confused.

"You two are going into hiding immediately. We have a place already—no one but my partner knows the details."

Scott rolls his eyes knowingly.

"Uh-huh—what about the dirty cops on your force that take their orders from Orlov and his kin? I heard plenty."

Harcourt points at Scott.

"My partner and I are clean—we don't take our orders from lowlife Russian types—and we don't tattle either."

Scott nervously looks at Carla.

"None of this is her fault."

Harcourt sighs loudly and shrugs.

"You two are marked until this mess is over."

He looks at his watch.

"There is something out there worth killing for and until whatever is being sought is found—lives are at stake."

He turns to look at the street again.

24

"I owe it to **Henry Morgan** to live up to his example of getting what he wanted without worrying about the risks."

Page **65**

Erik Smith looks at the photographs in front of him.

"There is a clue here somewhere."

Steve Andersen rolls his eyes and shrugs.

"You've been saying that for two hours and you're still no closer to knowing exactly what those old pictures mean."

Erik turns to face Steve.

"Supposedly the treasure that was part of Morgan's booty ended up being moved from off the coast of Jamaica after a series of hurricanes and earthquakes—and reburied somewhere in the British West Indies. According to credible pirate historians the whereabouts of what happened afterwards is uncertain."

He leans back in his chair.

"There's been talk that a band of pirates headed by someone named Long John Silver tried to find it but apparently they came away with nothing but a few pieces of scattered gold coins found washed up on one of the desolate isles in what is the modern-day locales of Tortola and Virgin Gorda. There was chatter that a cabin boy named Jim Hawkins stashed some of it from his pirate comrades but that remains a subject of dispute among historians and his own family. It was mostly forgotten until Gerald McCall apparently got his hands on some sort of map or object that linked directly back to the Jamaica story."

Steve seems bored and yawns.

"How did McCall come upon the truth?"

Erik looks at the house across the street and sighs.

"I don't know exactly."

He slides his fingers along the dashboard.

"If McCall gave it to somebody before he expired."

Steve looks at the photographs in Erik's hand.

"There's not much time left to get our hands on it before those scummy Russian thugs outsmart us to the finish."

Steve sighs loudly and gestures.

"Orlov and his men play without rules."

He runs his fingers through his hair.

"It's us or them—and I prefer it's us that come out ahead."

Erik nods in agreement and sighs loudly.

"Do you think Lorraine McCall knows?"
Steve looks at the house again.
"I'd place bets she knows something about what her uncle was up to. It would've been careless of him not to tell her."
Erik looks at the photographs once more.

25

"Who would do such a thing?"
Lorraine gasps.
"I'll be right there. Give me ten minutes."
She grabs her purse and runs to the door as Evelyn Hayes follows close behind. Seconds later they pull out of the driveway and turn onto a narrow street breaking the speed limit.

26

Vladimir and Bruce look back at the winery for a few seconds and get into their cars. Several yards away a huge pool of blood can be seen with a headless body lying in the center.

TO BE CONTINUED

A Brief Look at the Third Episode

A nasty surprise awaits a mobster as his rivals scheme to set certain events in motion while relationship issues test several people as pieces of a long ago puzzle begin to make sense.

Can You Hear the Laughter

1
Miami
Two Days Later

"I know it's quite a shock—but *surprise*."

Todd Whitney seems paralyzed as he looks at the young woman standing before him. Lizette Richardson grins broadly.

"Apparently your brother had a thing for black women. He liked dabbling plenty. Regardless, it's all legit. Check out the DNA tests for yourself—I'd be happy to take more if needed."

Todd runs his fingers through his hair.

"Calvin always had a wayward streak. Played with fire where Chandra Stevenson was concerned if I recall. The woman was a piece of work. She was killed by her lover's daughter."

Lizette rolls her eyes and takes a step forward.

"I know all about my half-sister. Rest assured I'm nothing like her. I've got my wits about me. I know how to play the game to get what I want. My mother certainly didn't raise a fool."

Todd leans forward and sighs.

"What do you want?"

"I thought it was obvious—I want it all dear uncle. Not just my share as you apparently seem to think is all I'm due—I want everything—yours—mine—every last cent—not a penny less—not a penny more—and unless you comply—things will get nasty."

Todd reacts in shock and leans back in his chair.

"Who do you think you are?"

Lizette pulls out her cell phone.

"Do you know where Thomas is at this exact moment?"

Todd shrugs. He seems bored.

"He's vacationing in the Bahamas with his family."

Lizette wags her finger at Todd.

"He *was* vacationing in the Bahamas with his family—as of one hour ago he's being held captive by one of my guys. Seems he got careless and didn't check to see if his bodyguard was actually one of his men or not. *Oops*—mistakes happen."

She points at Todd and laughs.

"One word from me and your precious brother will end up being fed to the sharks—such hungry brutes they are."

Todd clenches his fist.

"I'll crucify you."

Lizette rolls her eyes and smirks.

"Funny you should talk about such things."

At that moment two men force their way into the office holding a man and a woman against their will. Lizette laughs.

2

David Sherwood looks at his cell phone again and finally answers. He rolls his eyes several times. He seems annoyed.

"I thought I made myself clear—it's over."

He gestures with his hand.

"I never meant for you to get hurt."

He faces the balcony nearby.

"It was just fun and games—I'm sorry."

He looks at the cell phone in his hand several times.

"OK—OK—so hate me forever. Goodbye."

Page **70**

He runs his fingers through his hair as he shuts off the cell phone and sees Parker Ross coming toward him. He shrugs.

"Cassie's none too happy with me at the moment—she thinks I misled her. Said I told her we had something real."

Parker gives David a knowing look.

"Did you?"

David shakes his fist at Parker.

"I never told her I loved her. We were just friends—friends with benefits. She knew I wasn't serious—knew I played."

Parker takes a step toward David.

"Maybe you should rethink how you handle relationships that you assume is not going to lead anywhere—just saying."

David turns away from Parker.

3

Hugh Blandwick looks at Vladimir Orlov fearfully as he notices Bruce Copeland grinning broadly. He sighs loudly.

"I understand—I won't disappoint you again. I'm your guy from this day forward without hesitation. I'm ready to play."

Vladimir turns to look at Bruce.

"I think we need to test his loyalty—see if he's blowing smoke up our ass to avoid Tyler's fate. His time is money."

Bruce nods and points at Hugh.

"We have a job for you. This one requires nerves of steel to complete—sort of a way to prove how loyal you're willing to be to us—to our cause—our organization. Refusal isn't an option."

Hugh takes a deep breath and stands.

"I'll do anything—anything you demand."

Vladimir grins broadly and clenches his fist tightly.

"It seems that there's this woman who might hold the key to something we want. Bring her to us—scared but alive."

Hugh nods feverishly.

"Consider it done—tell me when and where."

Bruce shares a glance with Vladimir.

"Can we trust him with such a job? He lied before."

Page **71**

Vladimir laughs loudly and makes a slashing gesture with his hand. He points at Hugh and makes a slashing gesture again as Bruce nods in agreement. Hugh takes a deep breath.

"I'm your guy—test me."

They look at Hugh again and nod in unison.

"OK—Bruce will give you her name and address—bring her to us and you're one step closer to being able to wake up alive next week—fail to complete what we demand of you and we'll see that you end up in a landfill—without your fucking head."

Vladimir begins laughing.

"Do I make myself clear Blandwick?"

Hugh nods several times as he glances at Bruce.

"I won't let you down again."

Vladimir and Bruce look at each other.

"To make sure you don't get cocky and dream of skipping town I think you should know Bruce will be shadowing you."

Bruce shakes his fist.

"Are you still game Blandwick."

Hugh wipes sweat from his brow and nods.

4
New Orleans

"Are you still sore about what happened between me and your sister—I thought that was ancient history already?"

Cole Bouvier turns to look at Wesley Trudeau as they walk toward the open gates of an old cemetery. Cole stops.

"You slept with her a day before you got hitched."

Wesley makes a gesture with his hand.

"I never claimed to be a saint. Your sister and I had a moment and then it was over. It happened a decade ago."

Cole seems annoyed and shrugs.

"Uh-huh—and that's why I don't think you should ask her out. She really liked you—and then had to watch you take vows to be true to Candace. It took her weeks to get over you."

Wesley wipes sweat from his brow.

"Hey, I'm sorry about what happened. My marriage was a huge mistake. Candace Bordeaux was all wrong for me if truth be known. Our divorce is gonna be final in a month—over."

Cole stops suddenly as they both notice William La Porte coming toward them from one of the locked courtyards on the deserted grounds. He stops when he sees them and sighs.

"I'm glad you could come on such short notice. I got a call from a cemetery official earlier. Apparently from the records they kept concerning burials made in this cemetery there was a small wooden box that was placed with the remains of my great-great grandfather when he was buried in 1885. It's missing."

Cole and Wesley look at each other.

"What was in the box?"

William shrugs and seems confused as he faces the ornate cobblestone courtyard again. He nervously wrings his hands.

"I have no idea. According to the records, whatever was in the box was never disclosed. The casket was locked before it was placed inside the tomb—no one else in my family was buried in this cemetery after my great-great grandfather was laid to rest in 1885. His children were buried in another cemetery nearby."

Cole runs his fingers through his hair.

"What about his wife?"

William gestures with his finger.

"She remarried and was buried elsewhere."

Cole and Wesley share a glance.

"Can we take a peek at the records?"

William nods and leads them toward a narrow pathway leading to a modern-looking building several yards away.

5

"I'm not afraid of your father. Screw him."

Marko Prinze seems annoyed as he pulls Diane Singer toward him. He kisses her passionately. She giggles slyly.

"Daddy is just being a jerk. He can't stand to see me happy with anyone—made vile threats—said he'd blow you away."

Marko rolls his eyes and tugs at Diane's blouse. He pulls her closer to him. She giggles again as he looks at his erection pressing against his faded Levi's. He kisses Diane again.

"Seems to me your dad is just mad because he's not getting laid as often as he'd like—maybe he should find himself a hooker—someone that won't charge him a frigging fortune."

Diane seems disgusted at the remark.

"Ugh—don't go there with my dad. Like I don't even want to think of him touching my mother—they've had separate bedrooms for years now. My mother hates him—told me."

Marko rolls his eyes and groans.

"Your mother sounds like a present-day Scarlett O'Hara if you ask me—with the unhappy marriage included as well."

Diane looks at Marko curiously.

"Who was she?"

Marko reacts and sighs.

"She was a character in an old movie called *Gone with the Wind*—plenty of drama to be found. Misery loved company."

He looks down at his swollen erection.

"I think we both know what I'm thinking about at the moment. I don't think I can control myself much longer."

Diane wags her finger at Marko.

6

Miami

"As you can see I came prepared. There's no reason for pleasantries as far as I'm concerned. I want it—all of it."

Todd looks at Lizette coldly as she walks around his office while her henchmen grin broadly. In front of Todd a frightened man and woman stare blankly as the armed men seem ready to pull the trigger from each of their guns. Lizette sighs loudly.

"I've waited for this day ever since my mother let the cat out of the bag and told me that Calvin Whitney was my father. I grew up with nothing—never had anything—until now."

Todd stands up. He seems nervous and faces Lizette.

Page **74**

"I'm sure you and I can work something out—something beneficial to both of us. But first you've got to let my brother and his family go free—before someone gets hurt—namely you."

Lizette seems enraged at the comment and points at the women standing nearby. Without warning a gunshot is heard and the woman lies dead at her assailant's feet. Lizette grins.

"Strike one."

Todd glances at the man standing a few feet away with a terrified look on his face. Lizette takes a step forward.

"I'm not here to make side deals—I thought I made that clear earlier—I want it all—or plenty of bodies will pile up."

Todd clenches his fist and grimaces.

"I will not be bullied."

Lizette points at the man and seconds later a bullet rips through his skull. He falls to the floor. She faces Todd again.

"Strike two."

She winks at the two men standing with guns pointed at Todd. Lizette slowly walks over to where they are standing.

"Do you think I should mention to my dear uncle that I have his precious daughter in custody? Do you think he'd care if she suddenly ended up face down in a ditch just north of the city with a bullet hole in her head? Oh—such a pretty girl—it would be terrible if she could only have a funeral with a closed casket."

Todd reacts as Lizette faces him.

"My daughter has nothing to do with this."

Lizette wags her finger at Todd.

"Oh, but I think she does. If you refuse to play by my rules I'll have no choice but to follow through with my threat."

She glances at the cell phone in her hand.

"What is it going to be?"

Lizette begins laughing hysterically.

7

"I have no idea why someone would want to break into Gerald's crypt—he wasn't buried with anything valuable."

Page **75**

Lorraine McCall shakes her head as she looks at her sister while she shuts the door to her car. She seems visibly upset.

"Gerald liked history—never cared for money."

Evelyn Hayes looks at her sister and shrugs.

"What if he found something that someone else wanted badly enough to break into his crypt? What if what happened to him wasn't what it seemed? Maybe he was killed for something valuable he found? It's not like it would really be a surprise."

Lorraine seems confused and grimaces.

"But Gerald didn't want to be cut open after he died. He made us promise. Besides, he's been embalmed already."

Evelyn grabs Lorraine by the arm.

"So was **Tammy Wynette**. But a year after she died her daughters ordered an autopsy—left nothing to wonder about."

Lorraine seems uneasy and shrugs.

"Where did they take Gerald's body?"

Evelyn gestures with her hand.

"He was taken to the coroner's office. They wanted to make sure someone hadn't cut into his body to take out one of his organs for religious reasons—lots of that going around."

Lorraine seems disgusted and nods.

8

"I knew I could count on you Lizette. I'll call you in an hour to discuss what is to be done with Whitney and his daughter."

Houghton Fawcett leans back in his chair and begins laughing joyously as he shuts off his cell phone. He watches as his son comes toward him. They share a glance. Houghton grins.

"Todd Whitney is no longer a threat."

He snaps his fingers several times and laughs.

"Lizette has everything under control. As we speak he's being taken to a secure location—his daughter is already there."

Loren Fawcett glances at San Francisco Bay.

"What about Thomas Whitney?"

Houghton seems bored as he stands.

Page **76**

"Thomas Whitney and his family met a grisly end earlier this morning—seems their yacht exploded unexpectedly."

Houghton begins laughing and walks toward one of the large windows fronting the harbor. He turns around and sighs.

"The Whitney brothers have been a thorn in my side for years. They've controlled the East Coast for much too long."

Loren runs his fingers through his hair.

"I guess it's all yours now—yours and mine."

Houghton seems pleased.

"Eldon Whitney's death started a domino effect that led to Calvin Whitney meeting his maker in a small town in Maine brought on by his unstable illegitimate daughter. Luckily she was killed before she could cause us any real trouble. Now with Thomas Whitney and his family being turned into shark food this morning—the only remaining loose ends are Todd Whitney and his teenage daughter. Once I deal with them I'll take over the East Coast. I'll own everything—make everyone bend to my will."

Loren seems a bit confused.

"What about Calvin's other daughter?"

Houghton seems amused by the statement and begins laughing as he walks over to where Loren is standing. He grins.

"Lizette Richardson isn't Calvin Whitney's daughter. She doesn't know who her father is. I found her tricking not far from here and offered her a deal she couldn't turn down. Best deal I ever made with a hooker—that chick is a really fast learner."

He gestures with his hand.

"I dummied up some DNA tests for good measure and created this elaborate story about her youth. Todd Whitney isn't going to know one lie from another—he's been played."

Loren looks at his cell phone as it begins buzzing loudly.

"I thought DNA tests were really hard to fabricate?"

Houghton starts laughing.

"Money makes fabrication really easy to accomplish. Lots and lots of money can alter reality—Whitney is test of that."

Loren looks at his cell phone again.

"When are you going to kill Todd Whitney?"

Houghton waves his hand in the air and grins.

"I intend to keep him alive for now—at least for the next few weeks anyway. Seems he's involved with a stolen relic that is worth millions. From what I gather it holds info to where an elusive treasure hidden by **Henry Morgan** eons ago is located."

Loren runs his fingers through his hair once more.

"Wasn't he some sort of British pirate headquartered in Jamaica in the seventeenth century—a buccaneer of sorts?"

Houghton grimaces.

"That's his official title—but he was actually a brilliant adventurer who pushed the limits of society during that era."

He turns to face the window again.

"It was rumored he had a large stash of treasure hidden away before he died in 1688. It was subsequently moved to the British West Indies after an earthquake befell Jamaica. From there what happened to it is quite murky. Or it was anyway. Word on the street is that some two-bit historian found a statue in one of those old cemeteries in New Orleans and made off with it on the sly—rumor has abounded that it contained a map of where Morgan's long-lost treasure is presently located. Poor sap met a most unfortunate ending less than a week ago—courtesy of Whitney and his men. Unfortunately the whereabouts of the map remains unknown at the moment—or so it seems anyway."

Loren faces his father. He sighs loudly.

"Does Whitney have the map?"

Houghton clenches his fist.

"I'm certain he does. But no worries—he'll spill soon enough. Or I'm afraid his daughter will pay dearly for his sins."

They look at each other and nod.

9

"Uh-huh—I see. Wait until young Mr. Prinze is alone and pick him up. Bring him to me—he and I need to talk."

Eugene Singer grins broadly.

"Of course it means exactly what it appears to be."

He looks at the cell phone in his hand.

"I see great things in his future. A nice plot at Colma is certainly something to look forward to for a young man with such promise. Cemetery plots are getting harder to afford."

He dances a jig in front of his desk.

"Uh-huh—I think one of the Orlov brothers would love a task involving lots of pain—call Kevin Kulkovich too."

He nods several more times and laughs.

10

New Orleans

"Do you think they threw the box into the swamp adjacent to the cemetery? Certainly lots of trash there already. Place has become a dumping ground of late for appliances and bodies."

Cole runs his fingers through his hair.

"I still can't wrap my head around the fact someone actually opened a coffin and stole something from inside."

He watches as Wesley winces.

"Ugh—there's no way I would do something like that. No way would I dare want to look upon some guy with a skeleton face. It would be like a horror movie—one of those cheap ones you find airing really late at night—with bad creepy music."

Cole grins broadly and gestures.

"I think someone should check out the swamp."

Wesley turns to face Cole.

"Are you thinking what I'm thinking?"

Cole waves his hand in the air.

"Uh-huh—Delgado would fit the bill perfectly."

He looks at the swamp again.

"I'm still pissed at him over that incident with my niece. Said he was drunk—took her virginity and never called her afterwards. Claimed he didn't know what he was doing."

Wesley jabs Cole and laughs.

"Your niece is certainly no virgin."

Cole clenches his fist.

Page **79**

"She said she was—and I believe her. She's a saint if there was ever one. Violet is just friendly—likes to flirt with guys."

Wesley jabs Cole again.

"Uh-huh—tell that to all those guys she's friendly with down at Marvin's Pool and Beer. Face it—it was Delgado that got played—not the other way around. People talk plenty."

Cole seems irritated and turns away.

"You're asking for trouble Trudeau—especially after what happened between you and my sister years ago. I don't want her to get hurt again by the likes of you—once was enough."

Wesley digs his hands into the front pocket of his jeans and sighs loudly. He turns to look at the cemetery again.

"This thing with your sister is old—ancient—besides she can make her up own mind—especially concerning me."

He faces Cole and sighs loudly.

"I was there that night—Violet had her hands inside Delgado's Levi's. She clearly wanted to get laid. Took him home with her and pretended it was entirely his fault after the fact."

Cole shoots Wesley an angry look.

"I think we better get back to the station and get Delgado out in the swamp taking pictures with that camera he totes around all the time. If the box was dumped we need to retrieve it ASAP before it rains again—might still be fingerprints on it."

Wesley watches as Cole slowly walks away.

The Next Day

11

Scott Malone looks at the suitcase on his bed and sighs as he faces the balcony overlooking San Francisco Bay. Seconds later his cell phone begins to buzz. He slowly picks it up.

"Hello Roland—I was expecting your call."

He looks at the phone in his hand as loud yelling can be heard. He seems annoyed and shakes his head several times.

"There was nothing there. Stanley Ross is clean."

He gestures with his hand and grimaces.

"The dude is way in over his head with bad business deals but he doesn't know anything. Regardless I think there might be someone else that might. He mentioned a lawyer he knows."

Scott nods several times.

"Uh-huh—I think he might know plenty."

He runs his fingers through his hair.

"Already been down that road—he refused to talk to me when I called. Said he was too busy. Translated—he doesn't do interviews—made it clear. Face it Roland—it's over."

He grimaces as more yelling is heard coming from his cell phone. Scott seems annoyed. He glances at the bed.

"OK—OK—I'll give it another try."

He shuts off his cell phone and sighs loudly.

12
Napa Valley

"Such a way to go—imagine how this loser felt as his head was chopped off after being cut up like a piece of meat."

Bruce stifles a laugh as he watches the battered body of Tyler Fields being placed inside a body bag. Next to him Lance Moon appears upset and turns away. Bruce seems pleased.

"I bet he was probably in hock to the mob."

Lance turns around to face Bruce.

13
Washington DC

"OK—I see your point. I'll call you back in an hour."

Maxwell Pendergraft sighs loudly and leans back in his chair as he looks at the photos in front of him of a handwritten diary from the eighteenth century. He seems confused.

"What could this kid have found that people are willing to commit murder for? Plays out like a novel—or a TV movie."

He picks up one of the photographs and shrugs.

"What happened to your treasure Jim Hawkins? Where is it now? Who knows your secret? Is it someone I know?"

He reads aloud several passages from the diary and seems more confused than before. He rubs his jaw and sighs.

"I just don't see it. There's nothing here that leads to a clue. Kid just comments on hiding a chest full of rare coins."

He stands up and walks to the door. He stops.

"But what happened to the chest?"

Maxwell reaches for the doorknob seconds later.

14

"Where is the stiff now?"

Bruce gestures with his hand as he faces Vladimir with a sly grin. He begins laughing out loud as he sits down.

"At the coroner's office is my guess. They have no clue what they're looking for. Apparently the corpse was attacked by rats after we left—chew marks everywhere—ghastly."

Vladimir stifles a laugh.

"That bastard got what he deserved. His death will be a lesson to anyone who dares to go against my demands."

He pours himself a drink.

"Tyler Fields played his hand of cards and lost. It's as simple as that. I won't tolerate trash like him insulting me."

Bruce nods in agreement.

"What about Hugh Blandwick and his future?"

Vladimir takes a swig of his drink.

"Give him a few days. Give him just enough rope to hang himself—and if he pulls too tightly—I guess we'll know what will be his fate come seventy-two hours. Play on his weaknesses."

Bruce seems pleased and smirks.

"I want him for myself. I'm itching to put a bullet in his head after what happened last year—punk slighted me."

Vladimir laughs loudly and points at Bruce.

"How is Charisma Lawrence anyway?"

Bruce clenches his fist angrily and seems enraged.

"I dropped that whore after I found out she got played by Blandwick. He took her in the backseat of his car the night of your party celebrating Sergei's lovely release from state prison."

He turns to face Vladimir and points at him.

"I want that fucker dead—want him to know I'm the one who took him out for slighting me the way he did—bastard."

Vladimir smiles slyly and laughs.

"I guarantee it'll just be a moment longer. Blandwick is on his last days—Fields was the first—he'll be the second."

Bruce grins broadly as he clenches his fist.

15

Roosevelt Ross sits at the edge of a tiled pool as he sees his brother coming toward him. Lincoln Ross waves as he walks past a large garden of red roses. He stops suddenly.

"How about we go for a ride?"

Roosevelt gestures with his hand.

"I'm not in the mood."

He turns to face the pool.

"Do you think mom has a boyfriend already?"

Lincoln looks at his brother curiously.

"Why would you say something like that?"

Roosevelt gestures with his hand.

"I don't know—it just seems like a good reason."

Lincoln sits down near Roosevelt.

"They just grew apart. It happens. Some people just can't deal with each other when they get older—middle age."

Roosevelt shakes his head.

"I guess."

He stands up.

"Where's Parker?"

Lincoln shrugs.

"I think he and David stepped out for a quick bite—said something earlier about wanting to swing by Pacific Heights."

Roosevelt slowly turns to look at the house.

"Maybe we should visit dad at his office?"

Lincoln gives Roosevelt a curious look and nods.

"How about we get a bite to eat first and then surprise him with our presence. There's a cafe across from his office."

Roosevelt nods in agreement and follows Lincoln across the patio toward the house. They open the back door.

16
Washington DC

"Uh-huh—I'm aware of what he's been up to. I know exactly what I have to do when the moment presents itself."

John Berringer turns around to face Maxwell as he shuts off the cell phone in his hand. He takes a deep breath.

"Seems there's been a lot of odd activity since Thomas Whitney and his family met their maker in the Bahamas."

He runs his fingers through his hair.

"Todd Whitney is missing."

Maxwell gives John a curious look.

"Missing? Did he skip the country on his private jet?"

John shakes his head.

"Plane is still at the airport. He left his office yesterday with several people. None of them were on our radar."

Maxwell looks at his cell phone.

"Should we be worried?"

John gives him a knowing look.

"His brother just got iced and now he's nowhere to be found. If I were a betting man I'd say something is going on."

"Think he blew up his brother?"

John gives Maxwell a nervous look as his cell phone begins ringing. John looks at the name on the caller ID and winces.

17

"You'll never get away with this Fawcett. My people will hunt you down—tear out your heart and eat it with a fork."

Houghton laughs as he watches Anton Levitov tighten his grip on Todd's arm. He casually pushes him into the room.

"Oh, such dramatic wording from a fool who is helplessly tangled in my web—but no worries—your men as you call them know their place. They're on my payroll now. I call the shots."

He laughs loudly as he sees Todd's reaction.

"You and your brothers caused plenty of division on the East Coast with your tactics—made plenty of enemies."

Houghton takes a step toward Todd.

"But that's all over now. Both Eldon and Calvin met their maker several years back—and the terrible situation with that Chandra person resolved itself quite nicely. With them gone that only left you and Thomas—but as fate would have it your kid brother is scattered off the waters of the Bahamas. Of course that leaves only you and your daughter—at least for now anyway."

He points his finger at Todd.

"I'm not playing games with you anymore."

He clenches his fist.

"I want that damn map."

Todd stifles a laugh.

"I don't know what you're talking about."

Houghton signals to Anton. He watches as Todd's neck is twisted backwards. He screams in pain as Houghton grins.

"Shall we start over?"

He confidently takes a step closer.

"I know all about your quest to find the lost treasure left by **Henry Morgan**. Know all about your attempt to swipe the Hawkins diary from the Smithsonian. Know it was you that had that loser McCall poisoned. His death wasn't an accident."

Anton grins as he applies pressure to Todd's neck. He seems to be enjoying himself as Todd cries out in pain.

"Where is that frigging map?"

Todd winces in pain as Anton jerks him backwards.

"Shall we bring your daughter into this game?"

Houghton smirks as he looks at Anton.

"How old is your daughter again? Fourteen?"

He laughs as he sees Todd's reaction. He gives Anton a knowing look and laughs again. He faces Todd once more.

"I assume your daughter is a virgin."

He points at Todd and licks his lips knowingly.

"Anton is very sexually experienced with women—once your daughter loses her virginity to him there would be no turning around. She would come to know him very well indeed."

He grins as he sees Todd's reaction.

"Anton has a penchant for rough sex by the way—plenty of women have lost their virginities to him—learned to satisfy his needs—learned tricks—virginal girls are his favorite target."

Houghton watches with glee as Anton applies more pressure and laughs. They share a glance as Todd reacts.

"Leave my daughter out of this."

Houghton circles Todd and smirks.

"I don't know that I can at this point Whitney."

He reaches out and jabs Todd.

"You have something I want—but refuse to play ball with me. On the other hand your daughter has something Anton wants. He'll use his penis as a weapon—won't control himself."

Anton licks his lips and laughs.

"I'll make sure the path between your daughter's legs is heavily traveled by yours truly. She'll be quite the trick."

Todd struggles to free himself from Anton's grip. Seconds later Anton slams his fist against Todd's jaw. Todd screams.

"How long are we gonna play this game?"

Houghton watches as Anton prepares to punch Todd once more. Todd cries out and begs for mercy as he's hit again.

"There's no rest for the wicked as you know all too well. I want that fucking map and if I have to kill you to get it then that's exactly what I'll do. Of course there's that matter with your daughter losing her virginity to Anton. Who will protect her virtue once Anton breaks your neck? She'll be all *alone*—how sad."

Todd seems in a panic and grimaces.

"I already told you I don't know anything about a map. I'm as clueless as you are. Why would I lie to you? Ask yourself."

Houghton seems about to explode.

"How about sixty-five million dollars as a reason for you to keep your mouth shut. Uh-huh—I know exactly what that map is worth. You iced McCall after he gave you the frigging map."

Anton's grip on Todd's neck tightens.

"There was no map."

Anton twists Todd's neck even more and laughs.

"Is it worth your life?"

Anton begins applying more pressure to Todd's neck as he glances at Houghton slyly. Houghton begins laughing.

"Well? What's it gonna be—the map or your life? You decide. Either you tell me what I want to know or you'll be paying your dearly departed brothers a visit really soon. Time's up."

Todd looks at Anton and then at Houghton.

"OK—OK—it isn't a map. It's a key."

Anton and Houghton look at each other.

"Where the fuck is it?"

Todd shrugs.

"I don't know. McCall died before I found out where he hid it. I thought his people might know—but they didn't. At least they said they didn't. It must still be somewhere in his house."

Houghton gives Anton a knowing look.

18
New Orleans

Brian Delgado sits in a small rowboat and stares at the thick moss hanging from nearby trees. He rolls his eyes.

"Ugh—this place is a nightmare."

He looks at the camera in his hand and sighs.

"What the hell did Bouvier think I'd find here? Place is totally deserted. No one would dare step foot in this swamp."

He grimaces as he notices several birds picking at the bloated corpse of some sort of animal. He watches as they pick at the rotting flesh as the corpse bobs up and down in the water.

"I'm gonna be sick—several weeks probably."

He turns to look at a dock about twenty yards away and as he is about to look away he notices something stuck between a few strands of reeds several feet away from the wooden dock.

"I wonder what that could be."

Brian slowly begins rowing toward it as more birds descend on the swamp. He reaches the object and gingerly plucks it out of the filthy smelling water seconds later and groans.

19

"I think Bruce Copeland and I need to talk."

Lance sighs loudly as he looks at the scrap of paper in his hand with Bruce's phone number scrawled on it. He shrugs.

"Why would Tyler Fields have Bruce Copeland's cell phone number? Copeland never indicated they knew each other."

He looks at the piece of paper again.

20

"Where exactly is Prinze? I thought I made myself very clear that he was to be brought to me. He and I need to talk."

Eugene angrily walks back and forth in his office for several seconds as he listens impatiently. He grimaces.

"I don't give a fuck how many friends he has around him throughout the day. If anyone gets in the way you know what to do. No one gives a damn if some random teenager is found shot to death on the street. Do I look like I care? Find him."

He clenches his fist.

"I want him brought to me the minute you locate that wretched loser. He crossed the line with Diane despite being told to stay away from my daughter. Young Prinze needs to be taught a lesson—a lesson he won't forget. Once he's dealt with—Diane and I will have a long talk—whether she wants to or not."

He walks toward the window.

"Uh-huh—exactly what I was thinking."

He gestures with his hand and turns around.

"How hard could it be to find a horny college guy? He's probably at some diner adjacent to the college he attends. Get on it or I'll find someone who can. Of course if I have to find someone to do your job it'll look bad on your record with Orlov. I think we both know how unpleasant he can be when he's pissed off."

Eugene nods several times.

"Uh-huh—good—just so we understand each other."

He smirks as he looks at his cell phone.

21

Washington DC

"Uh-huh—thanks for calling. It fits perfectly. No doubt it hasn't been lying in that swamp for long. The wood would've already begun to rot. We'll be there on the next flight."

Maxwell nods several more times and shuts off his cell phone as he faces John. A sly grin spreads across his face.

"It seems that elusive clue we were looking for has just presented itself—in a swamp of all places—next door to one of those old cemeteries you always see on YouTube with people walking around clutching pocket flashlights at midnight."

John reacts and stands up.

"How do we know it's connected to the Hawkins story?"

Maxwell runs his fingers through his hair.

"We don't."

He shuts off his computer.

"I think I'll call Dirk Hawkins on the way to New Orleans. I'm sure he'd like to know those old stories he was told actually were true—with an ending worthy of a Netflix movie or series."

John grins and follows Maxwell out the door.

22

"This thing with Fields doesn't add up."

Lance looks at Bruce suspiciously.

"Why didn't you tell me you knew Tyler Fields?"

Bruce seems annoyed as he looks at Lance. He glances at the scrap of paper on top of Lance's desk. He sighs loudly.

"I already told you I didn't know the guy."

Lance runs his fingers through his hair and shrugs.

"I think this is something we should discuss with Chief Selby—something just doesn't feel right—especially given your spotty record of late concerning your recent hearings."

Bruce watches as Lance picks up his cell phone. Seconds later a gunshot is heard. Lance falls against a table nearby in shock. He looks at Bruce briefly, still not sure what's happening as he cries out. Bruce looks at the gun in his hand and smirks.

"Dead men tell no tales."

He slips the small handgun into his jacket.

"Got to remind myself to thank Orlov for lifting this gun from Tyler Fields after he met his end—sweet deal indeed."

He looks at Lance again and heads to the door. He closes it behind him. As the door closes Lance tries to pull himself up but doubles over in pain and begins gasping for air as he calls out for help while his voice trails off. He cries out for help again.

23

"What are we gonna do about Whitney?"

Houghton looks up from the report he's reading and grins broadly as he faces Lizette. He gestures with his hand.

"I'm not sure yet. He still has some value—but sooner or later he'll become a liability and will have to be dealt with."

Lizette smiles broadly and snaps her fingers.

"Anton wants to take him out as soon as possible. Wants a shot at Whitney's daughter too—thinks she can be useful."

Houghton laughs loudly.

"Uh-huh—I'll just bet he does. Nevertheless Levitov can be assured I'm fully aware that girl will serve us well on her back after he plows her—once her father is taken out of the picture of course—but first things first. I want that key found—find McCall's niece and bring that bitch to me—leave no stone unturned."

Page **90**

He clenches his fist and pounds it on his desk.

"I don't care what you do to that middle-aged nobody. I want that damn key found within the next hour or else."

Lizette nods in agreement and stands up.

<h2 style="text-align:center">24
New Orleans</h2>

"What about my family? I haven't told them I was threatened. I didn't want to scare them unnecessarily."

William runs his fingers through his hair.

"This all seems like a bad movie."

Cole shakes his head as he glances at Wesley.

"This is no movie. Those guys are serious. You're a marked man until they're in custody. They've killed others for less."

William sighs loudly.

"I didn't know I had relatives in England."

Wesley looks at the folder in his hand and shrugs.

"Uh-huh—Dirk Hawkins—the two of you share the same grandfather four times removed. He had no idea either."

William clasps his hand together.

"How did you find out?"

Cole grins broadly.

"It seems your records as well as those of Hawkins were linked together once they were digitized two years ago."

He hands William the folder.

"Apparently one of the daughters of Jim Hawkins married a man by the name of Worthington. He was a sea captain who regularly ventured to the Caribbean. They had two daughters, one of whom married a man from the West Indies by the name Pierre Jean La Porte. La Porte then moved with his new wife, the granddaughter of Jim Hawkins to New Orleans a few years later. It can be assumed he brought the treasure belonging to Hawkins with him and his new wife to the Crescent City. During the Civil War another marriage to Paul Le Beau tied your family to one of the richest families from the South—from there nothing."

Page 91

William seems confused and sighs loudly.

"What happened to the treasure? Where is it now?"

Cole gestures with his hand.

"That's the million dollar question."

He gives Wesley a knowing look and pulls out a small box made of wood with ornate carvings covering all four sides.

"We retrieved this from the swamp near the cemetery where some of your relatives are buried. It seems fairly old."

William looks at the box. He shakes his head.

25

"I'm not going anywhere with you."

Hugh grins as he pulls out a small handgun from his jacket pocket. He watches the look on Lorraine's face change as she realizes what's happening. He smirks and steps forward.

"I say you are."

He grabs her arm.

"It seems you have something we want."

Lorraine shakes her head.

"What are you talking about?"

Hugh notices Lizette standing in front of a car parked at the entrance to Lorraine's house. Hugh gestures to her.

"It's up to you. All of it."

Lorraine reacts as Lizette approaches. In her hand is a small blowtorch. She grins broadly as she signals for Lorraine to follow Hugh toward a blue sedan parked several feet away.

26
London

"I had no idea. It never occurred to me."

Dirk Hawkins reacts as he looks at Maxwell and John sitting in a room with William. He rubs his eyes. William waves.

"How did you find out about my long-lost relatives?"

Maxwell grins and points to Cole and Wesley.

"It seems in looking for items connected with the name Jim Hawkins they came across genealogy records pertaining to a long-lost granddaughter of which led to the gentleman staring back at you. This is your cousin several times removed."

Dirk seems in shock as he sighs loudly.

"I was told she died in a disaster at sea somewhere off the coast of Cuba. We assumed the entire crew was lost."

Cole flashes the folder in his hands.

"The ship sank but there were several survivors and they made their way to New Orleans—been there ever since."

Dirk rubs his eyes again.

"What happened to the treasure?"

Maxwell shrugs and gestures at William.

"That remains a mystery."

Maxwell and John glance at each other as Cole whispers to William. He points to several photographs of the carved box recently retrieved. William turns around to face Dirk again.

"Do these carvings look familiar?"

Dirk looks at the photographs as they are shown and shakes his head. He faces William again. He seems defeated.

"They mean nothing to me whatsoever."

William turns to face Cole and Wesley again.

"I was told that box matched the items buried with my great-great grandfather back in 1885. Could the records be wrong? Maybe it has nothing to do with the lost treasure?"

Maxwell looks at Dirk again and then William.

"There was something inside the box previously. Looks like it held some sort of statue or object of some kind is my guess. I'm assuming that's what the grave robbers were after when they desecrated your family's tomb and royally threatened you."

William turns to face Dirk once more.

TO BE CONTINUED

A Brief Look at the Fourth Episode

Secrets and murder play dual roles in the lives of multiple people as long-held secrets begin to unravel causing panic among many—while a key becomes the focus of several individuals.

Empire in the Air

1
Pacific Heights

"Where the fuck is that frigging key?"

Vladimir Orlov grabs Lorraine McCall by the neck and punches her hard in the face. He seems near his breaking point as he turns to face Sergei Orlov. They share a glance as he punches Lorraine again and viciously twists her neck backwards.

"I want that key or else."

He looks at Sergei again and winks.

"Really bad things happen to sweet middle-aged women every day in this country. Before the day is out you'll be on a slab at the morgue and I assure you it won't be a pretty sight."

He laughs loudly as he hits her again.

"Where did your uncle hide that fucking key? I know that bastard had the damn key with him when he met his maker."

Blood slowly drips from Lorraine's broken nose as she looks at Vladimir and Sergei. She slowly shakes her head.

"Please just let me go. I won't tell anyone."

Vladimir glances at Sergei and laughs loudly.

Page **95**

"Take her to the cellar. Do what you must to teach her a lesson for lying to me. Then kill her when you're done."

Sergei grins broadly and flexes his muscles as Lorraine seems terrified. He suddenly grabs Lorraine and drags her out of the room as he whistles a tune. Vladimir smirks as he watches them go. He shakes his head and playfully wags his finger.

"That brother of mine really enjoys his work."

He laughs again and picks up his cell phone. He seems upset as he begins dialing. He waits a few seconds and sighs.

"Even in death that bastard is still mocking me from the grave. Where did he hide that fucking key? Where is it?"

A few seconds later the line is picked up.

"Yeah—that's right I'm calling again. Seems that wretched McCall chick isn't going to be much help after all. Nevertheless someone knows where McCall hid that damn key and if I have to turn this goddamned city upside down I'm going to find it."

He seems irritated.

"I think it's time we find out what Winchester knows."

He makes a gesture with his finger.

"I agree—McCall's attorney knows plenty."

He hears screams coming from the cellar and smirks.

"I guess Sergei is introducing her to his penis."

He begins laughing again.

2

San Diego

"It appears that it's some sort of statue or other."

Harcourt Styverson slowly leans back in chair as he looks at Christian Malinger for a few seconds. He sighs loudly.

"According to what Pendergraft uncovered it seems that the treasure was buried and dug up several times. Word has it that it was dug up from where it had lain buried for more than a century on the island of Tortola and taken to New Orleans."

Christian seems confused and shrugs.

"Flood capital of the world?"

Page **96**

Harcourt gestures with his hand.

"Apparently it ended up at one of those old plantations that went bust after the Civil War. At that point the whereabouts of what happened to the treasure came upon a dead end."

Christian strokes his face for a few seconds.

"Do you think it's still there?"

Harcourt stands up.

"Who knows?"

He sighs again.

"I think we need to make a few calls."

Christian shoots Harcourt a knowing look.

"A trip to New Orleans this weekend is out of the question for me. I'm planning to visit my son in Ocean Landing."

Harcourt seems annoyed.

"I'll adjust if need be."

He reaches for his cell phone.

3

"I found this earlier by the pool house."

David Sherwood looks at the piece of paper in his hand as he reads it aloud. Lincoln Ross seems in shock as he listens.

"According to what this letter says your dad is deep in hock to some Russian dude named Vladimir Orlov. From how this is worded I doubt this Orlov guy is legit. Probably into all sorts of loan shark situations—of which people always end up dead."

Parker Ross walks over to his cousin.

"Is your dad in some sort of financial trouble?"

Lincoln reacts and snatches the paper from David's hand.

"This must be some sort of joke."

David and Parker share a glance and shrug.

"Doesn't seem like a joke—in fact it's downright scary if you ask me. I've heard stories about the Russian mob."

Parker makes a furious slashing gesture with his hand.

"They kill people for fun."

He lowers his voice and glances at the door.

Page 97

"My friends from Boston told me how the Irish and Italian mobs play sick games with people who cross them—but Russians are in a class by themselves. They enjoy killing their victims—and watching them die slowly. Your dad's in serious trouble."

Lincoln gives Parker a cold stare.

"My dad isn't involved with the Russian mob."

He looks at the piece of paper again.

"There has to be an explanation."

David gestures with his hand.

"Yeah—I'll just bet."

Lincoln looks at the piece of paper again and leaves the room seconds later without saying another word. Parker sighs.

"Maybe Castle Beach wasn't so bad after all?"

David rolls his eyes knowingly.

"Speak for yourself."

They turn to face the door.

4

"I'm almost done Sandra. A few more days, tops."

Scott Malone walks back and forth in his hotel room as he looks at the open balcony several times. He sighs loudly.

"Uh-huh—just a few more days—got to get additional details for my story. Roland insists upon it. Uh-huh I know."

He leans against the door to the balcony.

"He's being a dick without a doubt."

He gestures with his hand.

"I'll see you shortly."

He shuts off his cell phone and looks around at the room. Papers are scattered everywhere. Scott seems nervous.

"I wonder what they were looking for."

He looks at his cell phone again.

"I guess those idiots missed the memo that no one uses fax machines anymore—dopes are stuck in the 1990s."

He looks around the room again and sighs.

"Roland Parker has some serious explaining to do."

Page **98**

He begins feverishly dialing seconds later.

"I didn't sign up to get roughed up by a bunch of street punks with the morals of an alley cat—not my scene."

He waits for Roland to answer.

5
New Orleans

Wesley Trudeau shoots Cole Bouvier a curious look as they listen to Maxwell Pendergraft. He points to several images of estates in the New Orleans area. They seem bored.

"Those places don't exist anymore."

Wesley leans back in his chair.

"Those old plantation houses were razed decades ago to make room for housing projects throughout the city."

Maxwell shakes his head.

"What about the furniture?"

Cole stifles a laugh.

"That old junk got carted away to the city dump if you must know. Who would want to save anything from those old plantations anyway? From the pictures I've seen on the Internet that crap was ugly—unsightly—curbside garbage—all of it."

Maxwell sits down on the edge of the desk.

"Some of that stuff was worth millions—especially if one of those things was a mahogany chest with etchings on it."

Cole suddenly seems interested.

"Like exactly how valuable are we talking?"

"Millions possibly—tens actually in today's money if no one helped themselves when it was shipped to New Orleans for safekeeping. It seems our cabin boy Hawkins scored quite a bit of loot on one of his adventurous escapades to the Caribbean."

Wesley rolls his eyes knowingly.

"This thing stinks like one of those movies of the week that Lifetime tried to pass off for years as serious moviemaking. Oh-oh—what's next Pendergraft—a haunted house complete with a ghost that can walk through walls and talk—*oh my.*"

Page **99**

Maxwell seems annoyed and suddenly stands up.

"Are you two done with the dramatics?"

They look at each other in unison and begin laughing as they see his reaction. Wesley sighs loudly and stands up.

"OK—OK—how about we start over?"

Maxwell seems upset but nods in agreement.

6

Evelyn Hayes seems uneasy as she walks over to the heavy wooden dresser. From just under the right side she notices a small statue lying on its side. She bends over and picks it up.

"Ugh—I wonder where Uncle Gerald found this ugly thing—probably in some ancient crypt from darkest India."

She places it next to several other statues and becomes aware of a noticeable hairline crack along the back of the rust colored wood. Evelyn slowly picks it up again and sighs loudly.

"It must have cracked when it fell."

She gingerly slides her fingers along the back of the statue and suddenly it pops open. She seems shocked as she stares at a small exposed compartment. An old-fashioned skeleton key lies within. She cautiously reaches out to retrieve it. For a few seconds she stares at it unsure of what to make of it. She shrugs and looks around the room before turning to look at the key once more. A strange look comes over her face as she grimaces.

"I wonder what this is supposed to open."

She places it back inside the compartment and adjusts the cover into position. She seems uncomfortable as she continues to stare at the statue in her hand for a few seconds before placing it back on top of the dresser. Evelyn slowly walks to the door.

"Maybe Lorraine will have insight on Uncle Gerald's thinking for hiding a key in such a hideous looking statue."

She begins dialing. Seconds tick by but there is no answer from Lorraine. Evelyn shuts off her cell phone and sighs.

"Maybe she went to visit her daughter in Sausalito?"

She begins walking down the hallway and stops.

Page **100**

"Of course—why didn't I think of that before?"

She begins dialing in a panic and waits. Less than a second later the line is picked up. Evelyn leans against the door.

"Lincoln—can you come over—I need to talk to you."

Evelyn slides her finger against the cell phone.

"Yes—it's on Bridger Lane."

She takes a deep breath and shrugs.

"One hour will be fine."

She seems pleased as she shuts off the cell phone and glances back at the dresser at the far end of the room.

7

"She said she didn't know anything."

Erik Smith runs his fingers through his hair.

"Why would she lie?"

Steve Andersen seems annoyed.

"Oh, I don't know—it's not like women don't lie."

Erik rolls his eyes.

"Don't start with me about my ex-wife."

Steve makes a lewd gesture.

"Your ex was a slut—plain and simple—played you. Like deal already Erik—she had a well-worn path to her front door. There was more traffic between her legs on any given day than at one of those slick cheap thrill deals on Fletcher Avenue where the lines start from late afternoon and last until near midnight."

Without warning Erik punches Steve.

"That was uncalled for."

Steve rubs his jaw and grins.

"I'm just calling truth out—she made a fool of you."

Erik takes another swig from the can of beer in his hand.

"I loved her. She's the mother of my child."

Steve laughs loudly.

"What child? Your cousin was the proud papa."

Erik takes another swig of beer.

"Did anyone ever tell you you're a frigging prick?"

Page 101

Steve makes a lewd gesture with his finger again.

"Uh-huh—so what—ask me if I care."

He looks at his watch.

"I think it's time we pay Lorraine McCall another visit and shake loose her memory. She knows something no doubt."

Erik rolls his eyes and sits down on the sofa.

8

"What do you think it opens?"

Evelyn nervously turns to look at Lincoln.

"I was hoping you might know."

Lincoln seems confused.

"How would I know?"

Evelyn turns to look at Parker and David standing a few feet away. They shrug. Lincoln flips the key over and over in his hand. He seems lost for words as he faces Evelyn once more.

"I have no idea what this is for."

Evelyn seems disappointed.

"My uncle was quite weird—always collecting things that most everyone else would've discarded without a thought."

Lincoln glances at the skeleton key again and as he turns it over he notices some letters on the side. He repeats the words out loud as everyone seems confused at the meaning. He sighs as he looks at Evelyn. She glances at the key as Lincoln holds it up toward the light to see the lettering better. He faces her again.

"Does a Le Beau Court in New Orleans mean anything to you? This key opens something there—a safe probably."

Evelyn shakes her head.

"I've never been to New Orleans."

David glances at the laptop computer lying nearby.

"I'm sure Google would have plenty of info on Le Beau Court. I bet it's one of those old plantations where things go bump in the night—uh-huh—like some creepy old movie."

Parker reacts as he looks at Lincoln and Evelyn.

"I've seen enough creepy old houses to last a lifetime."

He glances at the others nervously and sighs.

"I'm not digging this key by any means—it probably opens a crypt or something—dried up bodies everywhere—ugh."

Lincoln laughs as he turns on the computer.

"Didn't you tell me a while back that Castle Beach had a bunch of creepy estates that was rumored to be haunted?"

Parker makes a lewd gesture with his finger.

"I don't recall."

He jabs Parker.

"Uh-huh—so says you."

They watch as his fingers fly across the keyboard. Within seconds images of a plantation fills the screen. Lincoln smirks as he glances at Parker and winks slyly. Several pictures pop up displaying various areas of the once-beautiful plantation.

"This seriously looks like one of those ancient places that the Discovery Channel makes documentaries about."

Lincoln faces David.

"No such luck here—place has been shuttered for over two decades. The park service has jurisdiction over it now."

He continues reading.

"It was owned by the Le Beau family for several centuries until twenty years ago. The last Le Beau—a guy named Michel Le Beau and his wife Amelia Roper kicked the bucket in a ghastly car accident right outside the front gates of the estate. I guess no one had to guts to tell a ninety-year-old man that maybe he shouldn't drive at night when his eyesight might not work the way it did previously. Anyway, from what it says here, the car was hit by an eighteen-wheeler point blank and the old folks went flying."

Evelyn seems upset.

"What about their children?"

Lincoln shrugs.

"No kids—none that were reported anyway according to the obituary—the estate ended up being auctioned off."

Suddenly an above-ground cemetery flashes across the computer screen. Several moss-covered tombs are visible.

"Are the Le Beau family buried on the property?"

Lincoln turns to face Parker. He winks slyly.

"I bet the place is royally haunted with spooks dating back before the Civil War era—plenty of tragic drama to keep the dead pretty active in places like this—lots of negativity for sure."

Evelyn turns away. The others notice.

9

Vladimir grins broadly as Sergei appears at the doorway of the kitchen. He notices blood splatters on Sergei's jeans.

"I assume you took care of Lorraine McCall."

Sergei laughs loudly and nods.

"That chick put up quite a fight—resisted my charms but I persisted like I always do with my girlfriends—and she and I got to know each other really, really well before I broke her neck."

He laughs again.

"I took her out to the city dump. No one will ever find a body among so much trash. She'll be forgotten soon enough."

He yawns loudly as he rubs his forehead.

"I think I'll go take a shower and hit the sack."

Vladimir nods in agreement.

"Tomorrow we'll go back to Gerald McCall's house and turn that place upside down—he hid that damn key somewhere inside that house—probably hid it in plain sight is my guess."

Sergei nods and walks away.

"I should've killed McCall months ago."

Vladimir clenches his fist.

"If I don't find that key I swear I'll kill his entire family."

He clenches his fist again.

10

Eugene Singer looks at the photographs lying in front of him on his desk. He slams his fist down angrily. He sighs.

"Take him out—Orlov wants him dead."

He turns to face Kevin Kulkovich.

"His family will know we mean business when they find his corpse face down in the pool. Kill his assistant also if needed."

Kevin grins broadly and leaves.

"That frigging bastard has played his last hand."

He leans back in his chair and smirks.

11
San Diego

"I'll have trouble sleeping without you lying next to me snoring lightly—don't do anything stupid in New Orleans."

Harcourt grins broadly as his girlfriend Juliet Malinger begins to unbutton his Levi's. He laughs and slowly pulls her hand away as she reaches out to kiss him. Harcourt sighs broadly.

"You know how much I love being with you Juliet—but I've really got to make my way to the airport in the next hour."

Juliet seems upset.

"I want you back in one piece."

She seductively slides her hand once again across his visible erection. He pulls away reluctantly and laughs.

"You'll be the death of me one day."

Juliet grins slyly.

"Men always say that when the sex between them and their girlfriend is really good—always playing the pity card."

Harcourt heads toward the door and stops.

"Best thing your brother ever did was set us up on a blind date last year. I've never been happier if truth be known."

Juliet suddenly runs up to Harcourt and hugs him warmly. They kiss for several seconds as tears run down her cheeks.

"I'll be waiting for you."

They hug again as Juliet wipes a tear from her cheek.

"When I get back we'll make up for lost time. I'll be like a caged animal—unstoppable—wild and unpredictable."

Juliet's eyes fall on Harcourt's erection.

"Stay away from all those loose women in the French Quarter—I won't say it twice—you're mine—I don't share."

Harcourt looks at Juliet oddly and begins laughing as he grabs the rollaway luggage a few feet away. He grins.

"I intend to buy plenty of condoms at the airport."

Juliet wags her finger at Harcourt.

"That better be a lie."

Harcourt winks and leaves.

12

"You're just gonna book us plane tickets for New Orleans without bothering to tell your dad where you're headed?"

Lincoln turns around to face Parker.

"Uh-huh—like what's the big deal anyway?"

He sits down on the sofa and looks at the skeleton key in his hand. David and Parker look at each other. They nod.

"This key thing might be way over our heads—who knows what that thing opens—might be a crypt. Ugh—I don't dig places where dead people are lying inside coffins—not my deal."

Parker grimaces as David winks slyly.

"I saw plenty of that in Castle Beach to last a lifetime."

David rolls his eyes.

"Castle Beach isn't New Orleans."

Parker gestures with his hand.

"Switch witchcraft for voodoo and it's the same actually."

David ignores the comment and slowly walks over to where Lincoln is sitting. He runs his fingers through his hair.

"What do you think this key actually opens?"

Lincoln shakes his head.

"No idea—no idea at all—but it must be something really valuable—probably a deed to an estate or something—or maybe some jewelry that belonged to royalty—possibly French."

David sighs loudly as he glances at Parker.

"What if whatever was stashed is long gone?"

Lincoln turns to look at David.

"You're quite the killjoy aren't you?"

David points his finger at Lincoln and shrugs.

Page 106

"I'm just stating the obvious."

Lincoln stands and walks to the window.

"I'm going—if you guys want to back out—go right ahead if it makes you feel better. I'll be back in a day or two."

Parker watches as Lincoln grabs a duffel bag lying on a table nearby. They watch as he dumps out several CDs.

"What about school?"

Lincoln stops.

"School starts next week—I've got four days."

Parker pulls out his cell phone.

"I think you should tell your folks."

Lincoln seems annoyed.

"That's what *you* would do—I'm not *you*."

He walks toward his bedroom a few feet away.

13

Chad Winchester winces as he's thrown against a cabinet at the other end of his kitchen. He looks up at the hulking man standing above him. Less than a second later he's kicked in the chest and dragged to his feet. Cujo Momoa grins as he viciously punches Chad in the face several times. Chad gasps for air.

"Enough already—Orlov has made his point."

Kevin steps forward from behind Cujo.

"You've crossed a line Winchester."

Kevin twirls a gun in his hand.

"Such sloppy behavior must be dealt with severely in order to make sure everyone knows exactly how we play. Tattling is an unforgivable offense Winchester. Did you actually think no one would catch on? Did you actually think Vladimir Orlov would let a slight against his character go unpunished? I think not."

He takes a step forward and signals Cujo.

"I hope your affairs are in order."

Chad watches in shocked disbelief as Cujo angrily forces him through the sliding glass doors that lead to a pool. Kevin watches the terrified look on Chad's face and grins broadly.

Page **107**

"Uh-huh—it's exactly what it looks like."

Kevin signals to Cujo and within seconds he forcibly pushes Chad toward the pool. Chad tries in vain to resist but is no match for Cujo's muscular arms and moments later he's forced to his knees. Kevin laughs as Chad begins begging for his life while Cujo sits on Chad's chest. His head is dunked backwards several times. He gasps for air as Cujo and Kevin begin laughing gleefully. Chad begs for mercy as his head is forced backwards once more into the pool. He continues begging as Cujo forces his head down again. Kevin turns away and signals to Cujo as Chad panics. A second or two later bubbles escape from Chad's mouth while Cujo holds his head under the water until his body goes limp.

"I bet he never thought it would end this way."

Kevin watches as Cujo stands up and throws Chad's limp body into the pool. They look at each other for a few seconds.

"Think we should leave a business card for Colma?"

Cujo gestures with his hand.

"I think it would be rude if we didn't."

They begin laughing.

14

Evelyn looks at her cell phone nervously and sighs.
"Where are you Lorraine?"
She seems worried and wrings her hand.

15

Scott is about to knock again when Stanley Ross slowly opens the door. He seems confused to see Scott. He shrugs.

"What are you doing here Malone?"

Scott looks at the folder in his hand.

"I had a few more questions."

Stanley seems annoyed and turns away as Scott follows him back into the office. Stanley turns around and sighs.

"I'm really busy. I thought I already made that clear."

Scott makes a gesture with his hand.

"Exactly what's going on with Vladimir Orlov?"

Stanley spins around to face Scott.

"I don't know anyone by that name."

Scott rolls his eyes.

"I think you do—in fact endless business lunches say otherwise. The question is why would someone as successful as you meet with someone that is basically lowlife pond scum."

Stanley glares at Scott.

"I think you'd better leave."

Scott looks at the paperwork again as he flips through the folder in his hand. He pulls out a second folder from his jacket.

"It seems to me you've been pretending more than usual lately. Your company is dead in the water and it's just a matter of time before everything else you've been doing catches up with you. What do you think Orlov will do when you can't pay him what you owe? Vladimir Orlov isn't exactly the generous type by any means—in fact he has a troubling rep for murder."

Stanley seems about to faint.

"This doesn't concern you Malone."

Scott takes a step forward.

"I can help you."

They look at each other.

"I don't need your help—I'm fine."

Scott wags his finger in Stanley's face.

"I guess I'll be hearing about the tragic fall you took off the Golden Gate Bridge in about a week or so—maybe sooner."

He turns to leave and stops suddenly.

"I know people."

Stanley points to the door.

"Get out and don't come back."

Scott nods and reaches for the doorknob. He sighs before closing the door behind him. Stanley slowly turns around.

"I've got to figure a way out of this mess."

He seems worried as he wipes sweat from his brow.

New York City

Sandra King rubs her eyes as she stares at the computer in front of her. She leans back in her chair as her eyes seem fixated on the Microsoft Word document on the screen. She sighs.

"Ugh—Scott was right about Serena St. John after all."

She glances at the photos of Serena and Houghton Fawcett standing in front of his yacht. She rubs her eyes again.

"But why would Houghton Fawcett and his son care about Tristan Montgomery Bell? Unless? Can it be true? Did Bell have something on Fawcett and his family that was worth killing for? Or was he part of their nefarious organization? But exactly how did Serena St. John become associated with people like this?"

Sandra looks at a mug of coffee on top of the desk and reaches out to take a sip. She leans back in the chair and notices several photos of Amanda Hardwick and Marlene Caswell at the far end of her desk. She seems confused and sighs loudly.

"If Serena was hired by Houghton Fawcett to entertain Armand and keep him away from his father as much as possible during Bell's Amazon trip—how does that explain Amanda and Marlene being on his yacht? They didn't have any ties to anyone there as far as I've found—why were they actually there?"

Sandra looks at the stacks of files nearby.

"This turn of events will keep my lawyer interested for hours—I bet he'll try to get me to drop the book altogether."

She looks at the computer again as her cell phone begins ringing. She smiles as she sees Scott's name appear. She picks up the phone and begins telling him about her discovery.

17

"He's dead—face down in his pool as you ordered."

Kevin grins as he watches Vladimir's reaction.

"I hope Winchester suffered before he met his fate at Cujo's hand. He simply wasn't worth what we paid him."

"He put up a struggle—but you know Cujo—he loves using his strength to make an impression on his victims. Winchester begged but it did him no good. He's no longer a problem."

Vladimir smirks and glances at the window.

"With Winchester and Fields out of the way I think it's time to focus on McCall again—and where he hid that statue."

Kevin makes a slashing gesture with his hand.

"Nothing came of Lorraine McCall?"

Vladimir laughs loudly.

"She's where she should be at this moment."

His mood suddenly switches to anger.

"Someone in McCall's family has that damn statue—and if I have to kill the whole lot of them to get it I will. That statue has a key hidden within—I want it—find it by any means necessary."

Kevin nods several times.

"Your wish is my command."

He turns to leave.

18

David and Parker watch as Lincoln walks toward them with plane tickets. He grins as he watches their reaction.

"Lighten up guys—this will be an adventure."

Parker nervously glances around the terminal of the airport. People are walking around everywhere as they seem oddly out of place. Lincoln runs his fingers through his hair.

"I left a message for the folks just in case."

David and Parker look at each other. David takes a step toward Lincoln. He curiously looks at the ticket in his hand.

"What should we expect once we get to New Orleans?"

Parker makes a barfing gesture with his hand.

"Lots of rotting bodies lying inside coffins no doubt is my guess. The smell will be horrible too—and for what exactly?"

Lincoln seems annoyed and looks at Parker.

"I already told you. Stop being a frigging baby."

Parker glares at his cousin.

Page 111

19

"It's not like her not to call me. Something's wrong."

Evelyn sighs as Irving Rivera rolls his eyes.

"I already told you on the phone I can't do anything until tomorrow. She hasn't been missing twenty-four hours yet."

Evelyn takes a step forward. Her rage is evident. She looks at the small office as she leans on the desk and faces Irving.

"If she were your relative or a fellow cop would you wait that long to start looking? I think not. In fact I know you wouldn't wait ten minutes before sending out a posse. Of course when it's someone else's kin you could care less about what happens."

"I don't like the tone of your voice."

Evelyn points her finger at Irving knowingly.

"You don't like the tone of my voice? Have you forgotten you work for me? You work for every citizen in this city."

She glances at the door of the office.

"It would really be a terrible shame if word got out how incompetent you were at doing your job. Elections are coming up Rivera—I'd think about that if I were you—losing a job as lucrative as this one at your age could really prove quite unpleasant."

"I think you should leave."

Evelyn faces Irving again and smiles.

"I expect you to start doing your job or I'll find someone else who can during the next election. Have a nice day."

She leaves slamming the door shut. He sighs loudly.

"Who does that bitch think she is? Doesn't she know who she's dealing with? Maybe it's time I talk to Vladimir Orlov."

He suddenly grabs his cell phone.

20

"Oh my God—Chad—this can't be happening."

Veronica Ross looks at the news coverage coming from her television and gasps loudly. She slowly turns around.

Page **112**

"Who'd want to kill Chad? Why?"

She seems in shock as she watches his wife and daughter standing next to a covered body. Several police officers and a coroner stand in front of Chad's wife asking questions. She shakes her head several times. Veronica turns off the television and glances at her cell phone lying on the small ledge in front of a large bay window overlooking Nob Hill. She sighs loudly.

21

New Orleans

Harcourt shuts the door to his rented car and begins driving out of the airport. He seems unaware he's being followed as he heads into the city. From behind him a blue sedan pursues him at a distance. He wipes sweat from his brow several times.

"It's been years since I showed my face here."

He laughs nervously.

"Oh the memories from college—spent so many nights in the French Quarter people actually thought I lived there."

He grins broadly.

"It was nice to be young and stupid."

He pulls up in front of a plain-looking brick building.

"Pendergraft said this was gonna be one of those cases where nothing is what it seems—then again he was always on the dramatic side—making things seem much more interesting than they usually were—always been his style—even in college."

He runs his fingers through his hair and smirks.

"I'll bet a year's paycheck that jerk still looks like he just graduated college—easily bagging chicks left and right."

He turns to look around.

"Damn pretty boys—always gets what they want out of life because chicks fall all over them—spreads their legs."

He sighs loudly.

"It would be funny if he was fat and ugly now."

He reaches for the doorknob.

Page **113**

22

"Do you think McCall's other niece knows anything?"

Steve turns to look at Erik sitting across from him inside their car. He shakes his head as he watches Evelyn enter the front door of her house. She seems visibly upset over something.

"It doesn't appear so."

Erik sighs loudly.

"McCall was a sneaky bastard. He wouldn't have told her anything for fear she'd stab him in the back down the way."

"But she was family?"

Erik jabs Steve.

"Do you think that makes a difference when it comes to money—lots of money? Have you forgotten what happened last year in Winter Bay with that family from Seattle? The wife killed her husband and two teenage sons—just so she could shack up with his younger brother who wasn't much older than her own sons. Case grabbed headlines everywhere. Cable news drained every bit of blood from that story for weeks. Wife got life for her vile crime—his brother got fifty to sixty—heard that there's a movie in the works as either a feature or miniseries."

He seems bored.

"This chick is as clueless as we are."

Erik looks at the house again.

23

Scott nods several times as he walks back and forth talking on his cell phone. He stops and faces the window.

"I told you Serena St. John was sketchy."

He waves his hand in the air.

"Nevertheless I think you've got a bestseller on your hands Sandra. Random House will be begging to publish your book."

He stops and looks at his cell phone.

"Uh-huh—I'm dead serious. Your story has everything that makes a tell-all rise to the top of the Amazon bestseller lists."

He shakes his fist in the air and laughs.

"No doubt about it—lots of intrigue and tragedy thrown together for good measure. Your book will absolutely be the definitive account of what happened to us in the Virgin Islands."

He nods again and grins broadly.

24

Houghton Fawcett leans back in his chair as he looks out at San Francisco Bay from his office. He sighs loudly and nods.

"Of course I'm glad that Bell had an unfortunate end in the Caribbean some months back. Uh-huh—I know. I agree."

He seems irritated and shrugs.

"He killed my son—bastard deserved what he got—but we had an agreement which I paid you handsomely for. I think that should count for something. The fact that two of your people ended up dead isn't a cause of concern for me—then or now."

Houghton leans forward.

"We had a deal—but things happened."

He makes a lewd gesture with his finger.

"Are you blaming me for Tristan Montgomery Bell losing his mind because some slug was screwing his trophy wife?"

He laughs and leans back in his chair again.

"You assured me that Serena St. John would kill Bell after Mayfield placed that photo of Bell's young wife and her latest lover in his office causing him to become unhinged. You said she would rub him out and blame it on one of his employees—some sad sack loser named Cooper Johnston. I had your word that she was one of your top assassins—that the whole thing would then be picked up by the supermarket tabloids and Bell's holdings would be worthless enabling me to easily snap them up."

He clenches his fist several times.

"But things didn't exactly go as planned, did they?"

He stands up and walks to the window nearby.

"That stupid old man snapped before he could be taken out by your people—Bell messed up everything I planned."

"Bell died when his yacht sank due to his own actions—so in actuality she didn't kill him like she was paid to do. If I wanted to nitpick I guess I could say Wesley Mayfield failed miserably as well in case it slipped your mind. From what you told me initially he was supposed to create so much drama on Bell's yacht by exposing the sordid dealings of Daphne Wade Bell that no one would know what was going on when her aging hubby got iced by one of your top people. Like I said, I think we're even when it comes to who owes who what. Nevertheless I like dealing with you, so yes, I'm open to any new business relationships you want to forge that could be beneficial. Uh-huh—I totally agree."

He looks at the cell phone in his hand.

"I agree—I'll see you in a week."

He nods and looks out the window again.

One Day Later

25

Diane Singer watches as Marko Prinze tucks his shirt into his jeans and faces her. He makes a lewd gesture and winks.

"I hope you've taken my advice."

"What advice would that be?"

Marko seems annoyed and he reaches for his socks.

"I don't want any surprises from you."

Diane reacts and sighs loudly.

"If you're trying to ask if I'm on the pill—the question is yes—I'm on the pill—religiously—you don't have to worry."

Marko stands up.

"A guy has to be sure these days—too many situations that can ruin his future when he least expects. Just yesterday one of my friends told me he was presented with a printout from some doctor's office. Yep—uh-huh—he's gonna be a daddy."

Diane pulls the covers around her body.

"I would never do something like that to you."

Marko runs his fingers through his hair and sighs.

"Uh-huh—so you say. Until of course you want me to marry you and be the kind of husband you always wanted."

He walks to the door and stops. He runs his fingers through his hair again. He seems upset and shrugs.

"You and I are just friends Diane—nothing more."

Diane nods in agreement.

26
New Orleans

"Are you sure this is the place?"

Lincoln turns around to face Parker as David stares at the broken-down estate a few yards away. David shrugs.

"Le Beau Court I presume?"

Lincoln nods.

"Uh-huh—Google Earth doesn't lie."

David faces the estate entrance again and sighs.

"I guess the government has better things to spend our tax dollars on—man, this place really gives me the creeps."

Parker watches as Lincoln steps out of the car and walks toward the rusted gates hidden by large shrubbery. He and David look at each other for a few seconds. David grins broadly.

"How bad could it be?"

Parker shoots David a nasty look.

27

Hugh Blandwick stares blankly at the computer screen and gulps. He reads the story again from an online newspaper and seems in shock. He slowly wipes sweat from his brow.

"Orlov's goons killed Winchester."

He glances at the door of his apartment.

"I don't want to go out like Tyler—Orlov crucified him and liked doing it. I'm a marked man no doubt—got to scram."

He slowly stands up and walks to the window.

"What do I do now? Where can I go?"

He nervously looks at his watch again and then at his cell phone lying on the sofa. He sighs loudly and wrings his hands several times before he walks over to the cell phone and picks it up. He cautiously begins dialing—then stops. He looks at the cell phone for a few seconds and then begins dialing again.

28
New York City

"Oh my God—it all makes sense now."

Sandra looks at the photographs of Amanda and Marlene once more and then faces the computer screen in front of her.

"They were on the yacht to get an exclusive interview with Victoria de Hoya for *Society Babylon*—and they pretended to be relatives of the de Hoya family in order to get aboard. Ugh—that tacky rag is even worse than the one Roland Parker owns."

She leans back in her chair.

"But why go to that much trouble for a lousy interview with Victoria? Why couldn't they just ask her point blank?"

She glances down at several headlines from *Society Babylon* focusing on the de Hoya family. She grimaces.

"Oops—scratch that. Uh—no wonder they were sneaking around the way they were on Bell's yacht—that story the year before comparing the troubled relationship between Victoria and her teenage daughter to the fictional one on *Knots Landing* between **Donna Mills** and **Tonya Crowe** sealed their fate."

Sandra glances at a photograph of Victoria.

"When my book comes out she won't be pleased with the turn of events I uncovered. Certainly isn't a pretty picture."

She taps her finger on the edge of the desk.

"I think she and I need to talk."

As she is about to pick up her cell phone she hears the front door opening and sees Scott standing there with a crooked grin on his face. She runs to him and they hug warmly.

"I'm glad you decided to come back early."

Scott hugs Sandra again.

"I missed having you next to me every night—pretty boring hugging a pillow like a girlfriend—weird actually."

Sandra hugs Scott once more and turns away.

"I've uncovered something about Victoria de Hoya."

Scott looks at Sandra curiously.

"Do tell."

Sandra glances at the computer.

"It seems Amanda and Marlene were reporters for *Society Babylon*—and they snuck aboard Bell's yacht on the sly."

Scott begins laughing.

"Kudos for them—I never had a clue."

Sandra jabs Scott.

"They took a page from your book of sneaky behavior in order to make Victoria look bad in print—exactly like Roland's scheme to tarnish Tristan Montgomery Bell's new marriage."

Scott pulls Sandra to him and kisses her.

"Roland Parker is bad—really bad. Deal with it already."

He kisses her again.

"Got a problem with me too? Think I'm bad?"

Sandra shakes her head and hugs him again. She sighs.

"I like you just the way you are."

He laughs and kisses Sandra again. She watches as his eyes seem focused on the bedroom door down the hallway.

TO BE CONTINUED

A Brief Look at the Fifth Episode

A mysterious key leads a group of college buddies to an abandoned plantation located in New Orleans where death stalks them at every turn and nothing is exactly what it appears.

Episode 5
Dark Mansions

1
New Orleans

Maxwell Pendergraft flips through a folder furiously as he seems at a loss for answers. Harcourt Styverson notices his desperation and gestures with his hand as he grins broadly.

"What's wrong Maxie?"

Maxwell seems irritated and faces Harcourt.

"Stop calling me Maxie."

Harcourt grins and stands up.

"You'll always be Maxie to me buddy."

Harcourt points his finger at Maxwell and laughs.

"That name defined you in college."

Maxwell playfully shakes his fist at Harcourt.

"I can still take you—bust you good."

Harcourt laughs as he slowly walks toward the door of the cramped office and seems amused at the threat. He grins.

"I've been working out plenty."

Maxwell rolls his eyes.

"Didn't you say you were starving?"

Page **121**

Harcourt reaches for the doorknob and smirks.

"We'll pick this up after lunch."

Maxwell points to the door.

"Buy me a roast beef sub—plenty of pickles."

Harcourt nods and leaves. Maxwell watches the door slam and shakes his head. He faces the folder on his desk again.

2

"Tear the house apart—spare nothing—I want that damn key found—it's here somewhere—I know it—I can feel it."

Sergei Orlov nods as he looks at the house across the street. He watches as Anton Levitov sighs loudly and clenches his fist for a few seconds. He seems more impatient than usual.

3

"Pick him up. Seems Blandwick has shown us what side he's on—bring that wretched worm to me this instant—alive."

Vladimir Orlov leans back in his chair.

"I said alive—I never said you couldn't rough him up. Knock some of his teeth out if you enjoy that sort of thing."

He laughs as he shakes his cell phone.

"Prepare two cement blocks. I think Blandwick just booked himself a pleasant fall off the Golden Gate Bridge."

He laughs louder as he looks out at San Francisco Bay and seems pleased with the turn of events. He rolls his eyes.

"Uh-huh—exactly what I just said. It'll be quite a moment for that two-faced backstabbing loser. Good riddance."

He smirks slyly as he happily snaps his fingers wildly.

4

New Orleans

Maxwell seems frustrated as he closes the folder. He looks around the office and shakes his head. He rubs his eyes.

Page **122**

"Hello Maxie."

"I thought I told you not to call me that."

He hears a laugh and looks up. He seems in shock as he sees Tiffany Johnson standing a few feet away. He reacts.

"Tiffany?"

She nods and takes a step forward. Maxwell watches her with a mixture of awe and fear. He takes a deep breath as Tiffany takes another step forward as time seems to stand still.

"Seems you're in a bit of a quandary, aren't you, dear Maxie? Looking for answers that remain somewhat elusive?"

Maxwell stands up and sighs.

"What's going on? What are you doing here?"

Tiffany rolls her eyes knowingly. Maxwell watches as she seems to stifle a smirk. She looks around the cramped office.

"I think you already know."

She takes another step forward.

5
Ocean Landing

"You wasted your time coming all this way. I told you I didn't want to see you. I haven't forgotten what you did."

Christian Malinger seems irritated as he looks at his teenage son. He reaches out to grab Jesse Malinger by the arm.

"I already told you I was sorry."

Jesse pulls away from his father and sighs.

"Uh-huh—I'll just bet."

Christian slowly runs his fingers through his hair. He looks up at the house a few yards away. He points at the house.

"Your mother and I had problems."

Jesse gestures with his hand.

"Was this before or after you slept with her best friend?"

Christian runs his fingers through his hair again.

"That's been over for years."

Jesse notices his mother standing by the entrance of a rose garden several feet away. He sighs loudly and grimaces.

"I think you know the way out of Ocean Landing. Don't come back. We have nothing to say to each other. Bye."

Christian seems in shock as Carol Malinger glares at her former husband. He turns around to look at his car.

6

Vladimir smiles broadly as he watches two of his men force Hugh Blandwick toward a waiting car. He laughs loudly as he watches two other men toting cement blocks. He shakes his head as he faces Loren Fawcett. He points and smirks.

"When they find his miserable corpse it'll take plenty of work to match his dental records if they ever find him at all."

Loren nods in agreement.

"Any word from New Orleans yet?"

Vladimir shakes his head and seems worried.

"Something must have gone wrong—or else those two relatives of ours are playing both sides hoping to outsmart us."

Loren wags his finger at his cousin.

"They wouldn't dare."

Vladimir turns to look at Hugh again. He cries out for mercy as he notices the cement blocks. Vladimir laughs.

7
New Orleans

"Mind telling me how you came upon this little piece of info—less than an hour ago you told me you had nothing."

Harcourt notices Maxwell's weird reaction to his comment and reaches out to grab his arm as they walk toward a parked car several feet away. Maxwell faces Harcourt and shrugs.

"You wouldn't believe me if I told you."

Harcourt seems confused.

"What's that supposed to mean?"

Maxwell looks back at the building and for a second notices a teenage girl looking out one of the windows.

"How about we discuss it later? We don't have much time from what I was told. Lives are at stake—several in fact."

Harcourt seems annoyed and sighs loudly.

"You haven't changed one bit since we were in college. Always keeping secrets—endlessly playing mind games."

Maxwell gets into the car and grins.

8

Eugene Singer clenches his fist as he watches Marko Prinze slam the door to his car and head toward a bar.

"That loser is in for a world of hurt."

He grabs his cell phone and begins dialing.

"Uh-huh—I've got my eye on Prinze as we speak. Come to Sixth and Nob Hill pronto. Someone is gonna take a ride."

He laughs as he looks at the bar again.

9
New Orleans

David Sherwood and Parker Ross gingerly walk toward the front entrance of an abandoned estate. Dried leaves crunch under their feet as they look around every few seconds. Lincoln Ross pulls out his cell phone and winces as he sees several images appear on the screen. He shows it to Parker. They react.

"There's a swamp nearby. A bog actually."

David stops and faces them.

"I'm not digging this place one bit."

Lincoln jabs David.

"Tell me something I don't already know."

They face the entrance of the old estate again as their eyes seem to play tricks on them. Several loud sounds are heard in a distance—gunshots to be exact. Parker stops suddenly.

"What was that?"

Lincoln rolls his eyes.

"What does it sound like cousin?"

He pushes Parker forward as David follows.

"Maybe this wasn't such a good idea. How about we call it a day—tell your former teacher we struck out—found nothing."

Lincoln knowingly shakes his fist at Parker.

10

"I need more time—a week perhaps. It's the best I can do on such short notice. I'm true to my word. I'm good."

Stanley Ross shakes his head as he walks back and forth in his office talking on his cell phone. He stops suddenly.

"That was uncalled for. I said I'd pay."

He sighs loudly.

"I'll call you tomorrow."

Stanley nods several times and turns around.

"My word is my bond Vladimir."

He nods again and shuts off his cell phone. His gaze falls upon a folder on his desk. Stanley wipes sweat from his brow.

"Why did I ever let myself get into business with the Orlov brothers—and Houghton Fawcett? The man is no good."

He runs his fingers through his hair.

11
Ocean Landing

"You didn't have to be so hard on him."

Jesse turns to look at his mother and gestures with his hand as he turns to look at the empty street again. He sighs.

"Uh-huh—I did. He needs to learn a lesson from what he did to you—to us. Or he'll repeat his behavior ten plus."

Carol gives her son a curious look.

"When did you become so smart about life?"

Jesse rolls his eyes at his mother.

"I watch the news a lot—plenty of idiots in the world."

Carol looks at the street again and then at Jesse. They slowly walk toward the front steps of their Victorian home.

12

"Are you sure that Evelyn Hayes told us the truth about McCall's statue? How do we know she wasn't lying to us?"

Vladimir turns to face Loren as they look at several photos of a New Orleans cemetery. He wags his finger and seems pleased with the turn of events. He grins broadly and sighs.

"I threatened to kill her unless she came clean. That bitch believed I'd let her live after everything that happened."

He laughs loudly and jabs Loren playfully.

"I broke her neck right after and then made a call to William La Porte. Made it clear what lays ahead for him too."

He jabs Loren again and grins.

"We also took out two guys named Smith and Andersen that we found hanging around McCall's former home."

He makes a lewd gesture with his finger.

"They were connected to Gerald McCall no doubt."

He smirks as he sees Loren's reaction.

"Chill out. This New Orleans deal will reap rewards for us the minute we find what that key unlocks. Your dad will owe us royally—he'll be indebted to us—show us proper respect."

Loren seems nervous as he looks at his fingers.

"Last time you said that my father lost millions. Said it was we who owed him afterwards—not the other way around if you recall Vladimir—made it clear he owned us body and soul."

Vladimir gestures with his hand and shrugs.

"That was then—this is now."

Loren seems worried and sighs loudly.

13
New Orleans

"Uh-huh—I'm on my way as we speak Pendergraft. Your timing couldn't be worse if you tried. Just about to score with a hot number I met an hour ago in the French Quarter."

Page **127**

"How much is she charging for her services?"

John Berringer seems annoyed as he glances at his cell phone and sees Maxwell grinning broadly. He looks back at a parking lot as a woman blows a kiss to him. He sighs loudly.

"Like I would have to pay for a roll in the hay? She's no hooker—just a young woman who wanted to get into my pants and give me a thrill. Create some memories for yours truly."

"What about Sophia?"

He shakes his fist at Maxwell.

"Sophia Vanek and I cooled it last week—something about me not wanting to commit to walking down the aisle."

Maxwell wags his finger John.

"Uh-huh—likely story—plenty of holes to patch up in that story if I do say so myself—especially knowing your rep."

John reacts to the slight.

"I'll see you in a half hour or so."

Maxwell nods and the screen goes blank on John's cell phone. He sighs loudly as he opens the door to his car.

14

Roosevelt Ross is sitting on the sofa watching an episode of one of the seasons of *Amazing Race Canada* when a news alert is made about the grisly finding of a woman's battered body at the home of her late uncle. He leans forward and turns up the volume as details are made connecting her murder with her late uncle's death. Roosevelt seems worried as he glances at his cell phone a few feet away on the coffee table. He sighs loudly.

"Why does that woman's name seem so familiar to me?"

He grabs the cell phone and begins dialing.

15
New Orleans

"Where is La Porte now? I thought I told him to stay put until we caught the punk that threatened him—damn it."

Page **128**

Wesley Trudeau turns to look at Cole Bouvier sitting across from him with his feet on top of his desk. He shrugs.

"I'm on my way—meet me in the parking lot."

He shuts off his cell phone and shoots Cole a strange look at he grabs his jacket. He runs his fingers through his hair.

"Seems La Porte just got a call from Maxwell Pendergraft about something going down at that old estate we sent Delgado out to investigate previous. Trouble is brewing no doubt."

Cole jumps up and grabs his jacket.

"Where's Delgado?"

Wesley faces Cole and sighs.

"He's waiting for us. Got a couple other guys with him from what he said—plenty of gun action if need be."

They shut the door behind them.

16

"You won't get away with this—they'll catch you. I know the law—you'll fry. My dad won't rest until you're toast."

Eugene looks at Marko sitting in a chair a few feet away from him. Duct tape binds Marko's arms and legs to a chair as Eugene begins laughing. He points at Marko and smirks.

"I warned you to stay away from my daughter—but you defied me anyway. Dared me to act—insulted me."

He reaches out to grab Marko's jaw.

"This is the end of the road for you young man. Your time has run out. Hope your father has space for you in the family plot at Colma—a closed casket funeral—no news coverage."

Marko tries to free himself from his restraints as Eugene signals to Bruce Copeland standing nearby. Bruce grins broadly as he looks at a syringe in his hand. He waves it in the air.

"You'll pay. I swear you will."

Eugene points to Marko and laughs.

"It's you who's gonna pay young man—one shot from this needle and you'll be in a whole new world—I guarantee it."

Bruce smirks as he takes a step forward.

"They'll find your bloated corpse in one of those alleys frequented by junkies—just another loser—nothing more."

He and Eugene share a look and begin laughing. Marko again tries to push against his restraints. He sighs loudly.

"Not everything is what it appears Singer—you'll see."

Eugene seems annoyed at the comment.

"Enough with this prattle Prinze. Colma is waiting."

Without warning Bruce leaps at Marko and plunges the syringe in his hand into Marko's arm. Marko reacts. Less than a second later he begins to shake uncontrollably as foam begins coming from his mouth. His eyes roll over in their sockets as he continues to shake violently. Eugene and Bruce burst into laughter as they watch Marko's last seconds of life ebb away.

17

"Oh my God—how could he—oh sweet Marko."

Diane Singer screams as she watches in shocked disbelief at the live streaming video coming from Marko's cell phone.

"He's going to pay for this—they both will."

She clenches her fist as she watches her father and Bruce stand next to Marko's limp body as they continue laughing.

18
New Orleans

Maxwell stands by his car parked at the entrance of a broken down estate. Harcourt shakes his head and sighs.

"Apparently Le Beau Court was once the envy of everyone in this area—wouldn't know it now by the looks of it—sad."

Maxwell rolls his eyes knowingly.

"Estates like this cost money to maintain—hard times usually spell the end for such things—a relic of the past."

Harcourt looks at the entrance again.

"Where do you think Berringer is at the moment?"

Maxwell shakes his head and grins broadly.

"He's probably still pissed that I rained on his parade to get laid while he's hanging in the Crescent City for a spell."

Harcourt makes a lewd gesture with his finger.

"Guys like you and John are always looking for the latest flavor. I bet he was as wild as you were in college—lost count of all the girls he bedded every weekend—spent a fortune in condoms at the local drugstore—lied about being faithful."

Maxwell wags his finger at Harcourt.

"Do I sense a tinge of jealousy in your voice?"

At that moment John pulls up. Right behind him Wesley and Cole show up along with Brian Delgado. Several other police officers step out of their cars as well. Maxwell seems confused as they come toward him. He glances briefly at the entrance to the estate as another car pulls up seconds later. He sighs loudly.

19

Lizette Richardson watches as Anton licks his lips several times as he looks at a live streaming monitor of Bridget Whitney in a private room inside Houghton Fawcett's mansion. She smiles knowing what he's thinking. She jabs him several times as she notices his erection straining against his faded Levi's. He turns to face her. He looks down at his swollen erection and laughs.

"I want her—want her virginity—and I intend to have a party the moment Houghton gives me the word. She'll be a believer no doubt. She'll be turning tricks soon enough."

Lizette jabs Anton again knowingly.

"I thought you promised to be true to me."

Anton looks at Lizette and begins laughing as he glances at the monitor briefly. He faces Lizette again and smirks slyly.

"You've got quite the sense of humor."

He looks at his cell phone.

"Not sure why Fawcett wants to keep Whitney alive. That man is worth more to us with a bullet in his head. As long as he's breathing he poses a threat—not sure what Fawcett's ultimate goal is concerning his one-time rival—makes no sense."

Lizette strokes Anton's shoulder lightly and faces the monitor again. She then reaches out to hug him warmly.

"Don't worry about Fawcett's motives. I assure you, you'll get your shot at Todd Whitney when the moment calls for action. Houghton Fawcett knows you want to take Whitney out—knows how much you dislike your former boss—knows your deal."

Anton clenches his fist and grimaces.

"That man played me for a fool—set me up to take the fall for killing his ex wife. Paid me to sleep with her and then tried to make it look like her falling from the balcony of Whitney's condo was my doing. Imagine my surprise when the cops picked me up and tried to say it was me that killed the recently divorced wife of a mobster with plenty of cops on the payroll. I would've fried if it hadn't been for the fact I had been seeing my brother's ex on the sly. She cleared me—provided video that she and I were in Chicago the day of the accident. Whitney had her murdered a week later—made it look like she was killed in a car accident."

Lizette reaches out to stroke Anton's arm.

"Todd Whitney is a piece of work no doubt. That whole family was royally messed up. His older brothers killed their rivals in the most violent ways—one of them going so far as to have his former accountant fed to a lion while on an African safari."

Anton rolls his eyes.

"It wasn't a lion—it was a leopard."

Lizette looks at the monitor again and shrugs.

20

Diane looks at the gun in her hand and smiles as she slides her fingers over the trigger. She turns to look at the window.

"Daddy dear, you'll regret forcing me to take shooting lessons last year. Seems you and I have plenty to discuss."

She walks to the door and opens it. She stops.

"But first things first—Bruce Copeland and I need to have a serious talk about Marko. I wonder how he likes surprises."

She glances at her cell phone and sighs loudly.

Page 132

21

New Orleans

"Who do you think they are? What do they want?"

Lincoln turns to look at Parker with disdain as they watch several men walking around the abandoned estate as if looking for something. David nervously runs his fingers through his hair as he notices one of the men appears to be carrying a gun.

"What do we do now?"

Lincoln turns to face David and shrugs.

"Wait and see what they're up to. Could be from some stupid ghost hunting show—the ones where everyone pretends to be talking to dead people but in reality they're just faking the whole thing. I bet that's why these jokers are here—trying to mooch off all the other shows that already filmed here."

Parker gives Lincoln a knowing look.

"Uh-huh—then why do they have guns? Are they planning to shoot one of the ghosts you claim is smoke and mirrors?"

At that moment David feels something touch him on the shoulder. He turns around but sees nothing. He reacts.

"Something just touched me."

Lincoln and Parker look at David and laugh.

"Uh-huh—good one—save it for *People* magazine."

David seems annoyed and looks around.

"I know what I felt—something touched me."

Lincoln and Parker begin laughing again and realize the men they were looking at seconds ago are now walking towards them. They look around for an escape route and see none.

22

"He's gonna turn that poor girl inside out when he's done with her. There won't be anything left for her to dream about."

Lizette smiles as she watches Anton opening the door to Bridget's room. Anton's laughter echoes as he shuts the door.

"You and I are gonna get to know each other really well and then some—seems your father left you in my care."

Lizette watches the video as it continues to stream while Anton circles Bridget like a hunter about to kill his prey. She backs away from him and seems terrified as he grabs hold of her. He pulls her toward him and laughs again. Anton rips her skirt off seconds later and forces her up against the door. Lizette watches in fascination as she realizes Anton's erect penis is sticking out in front of him. She shakes her head as she watches the look on the teenage girl's face realizing what is about to happen. Less than a second later Anton forces his penis between her legs and begins raping her. He laughs loudly as the rhythmic thrusting of his hips leaves nothing to the imagination. Bridget cries out in shock but that only seems to excite Anton further as he plows her with even more urgency. Lizette smiles broadly as she continues to watch the live action adult movie play out in front of her. She sighs.

"That girl is gonna work out just fine for what Houghton Fawcett has in store for her—she'll be in demand from every guy in Fawcett's employ with a frigid wife. She'll be traded repeatedly for the first couple of years. Eventually she'll become old news and will be discarded like so many before her. Oh well."

She turns off the monitor as Bridget's screams continue to echo as Anton intensifies his assault. The screen goes blank.

23
New Orleans

Maxwell appears confused as he sees Tiffany standing directly behind David. He watches her reaction and realizes David isn't aware that she's standing next to him. He glances at Lincoln and Parker and then at Harcourt and John just a few feet away. In a distance an old cemetery is clearly visible behind an iron gate covered with long-dead moss. He shoots Tiffany a cautious look as she points to the driveway of the estate. He rolls his eyes.

"OK—so let's play this story out again shall we. How exactly did you three happen to come across said statue?"

Lincoln turns to look at William La Porte.

"How about you tell us again exactly how this statue is connected to some old dead sailor named Jim Hawkins."

"He was a distant relative of mine from what I've been told. He happened across buried treasure somewhere in the British Virgin Islands during the eighteenth century."

Maxwell appears to be annoyed and sighs loudly. He steps in front of William and faces Lincoln. They look at each other.

"I'm asking the questions—not you."

Lincoln turns to look at David. He waves his hand in the air and pretends to be Maxwell by imitating his behavior.

"Can you believe this guy—he thinks because he says he's FBI we'll just fall in line and tell him everything we know."

At that moment they notice Wesley and Cole gesturing to Brian. Le Beau Court looms above them as silence permeates the area for a few seconds. Lincoln points at Wesley and Cole.

"Didn't know there would be a show?"

Maxwell shoots Wesley a knowing look as he faces Lincoln again. He points at the cemetery in a distance and shrugs.

"Where is the frigging key you said was hidden inside the statue you came upon through one of your teachers?"

Lincoln gestures with his finger and grins.

"I've decided to take the fifth."

Maxwell realizes Tiffany is no longer there.

"Give me the frigging key."

Lincoln nervously glances at Maxwell and turns to look at David and Parker. They shake their shoulders in unison.

"I'm not going to ask again."

Lincoln reaches into the pocket of his Levi's.

24
London

Dirk Hawkins looks at the images of Le Beau Court on the screen of his computer. He shakes his head several times as a misty fog hovers over the abandoned estate. He sighs loudly.

Page **135**

"That place gives me bad vibes. Looks like something right out of a gothic soap opera with a Halloween theme."

He turns to look at a folder containing scanned images from the diary of Jim Hawkins and shakes his head again.

"What other secrets does my family not know about concerning that treasure chest you found so long ago?"

He reaches out and grabs his cell phone. Dirk dials and waits for a few seconds but there's no answer. He shuts off the phone and seems nervous as he looks at the computer again.

25

A huge grin blankets Anton's face as he looks at Bridget lying on the floor. She seems in shock. He laughs loudly.

"You and me—we're quite a pair."

He looks at his exposed penis and smirks.

"Uh-huh—I think a second round is certainly something I can rise to the occasion for—wish your father could see us now doing the nasty after he forbid me from looking at you."

He begins laughing and roughly grabs her.

26

"Singer is on cloud nine after what just took place with that punk kid. Jerk had it coming no doubt—paid dearly."

Bruce reaches out to grab the back door of his house as a clicking sound can be heard. He turns around and reels in shock as two bullets pierce his chest. A few feet away Diane looks at the gun in her hand—touches the silencer lightly and smiles.

"One down—one to go—hope daddy is planning for a shocker—he's certainly earned it after what he did to Marko."

Diane turns and walks calmly down the sidewalk. A few people jog past her but see nothing unusual. She smiles as she pulls out her cell phone and begins dialing. She sighs loudly.

"Uh-huh—daddy—I need to see you."

She nods briefly and shuts off the cell phone.

Page 136

"I'll take that if you don't mind young man."

Thick mist covers Le Beau Court as Igor Levitov and then Sasha Levitov slowly approach—each holding machine guns.

"I think you have something that belongs to us."

Maxwell and Harcourt seem in shock as they watch the scene unfolding. Wesley and Cole share a look while Brian and William react as the two men raise their machine guns.

"One wrong move and you guys will resemble Swiss cheese covered in ketchup—minus the soft touch of course."

Igor smirks as he glances at the key in Lincoln's left hand.

"I'm going to count to three."

He gives Sasha a knowing look.

"Then you die."

Lincoln glances at Parker and David and then at Maxwell nervously. At that moment a cloudy wisp of cold air blows past them while Igor reacts as if something just touched him.

"What the fuck?"

Maxwell reacts as he sees Tiffany standing directly behind Igor. She smiles broadly and gestures. Seconds later her hands wrap around Igor's throat. As she begins violently choking him he drops his machine gun and panics. She intensifies her grip on his throat as Sasha seems confused about what Igor is reacting to at that moment. Maxwell looks at the others and realizes they can't see Tiffany. He faces her again just as Igor begins crying out while Tiffany's invisible hands squeeze tighter and tighter around his neck. Igor looks toward Maxwell and screams for help.

"There's something here—some *creature*."

He tries to push Tiffany away as he begins gasping still unable to free himself. He falls to his knees as everyone remains frozen as they look at the strange scene playing out. Sasha looks at the machine gun in his hand and then at the others.

"There's nothing here Igor. I can't see anything."

He takes a step toward Igor while keeping the gun pointed at his prey. They remain frozen where they stand. It is at that moment Maxwell realizes Tiffany isn't alone anymore. As he watches unable to move he looks at the events unfolding in front of him and the others. Jeremy Weissmann materializes and takes hold of Sasha. Sasha screams in fright and drops the machine gun as invisible hands begin to tighten around his neck. He begs for help as Maxwell continues watching in fascination as Tiffany and Jeremy look at him briefly. Igor manages to escape from Tiffany's grasp and seems spooked as he looks around unable to speak. Without warning he takes off running toward the entrance of the abandoned estate. Sasha watches Igor run frantically into the thick mist and panics. He begins begging for mercy as Jeremy glances at Tiffany and they nod in agreement once more.

"Are you seeing this freak show?"

Lincoln turns to look at Parker and David standing next to him. They look at him but say nothing. Wesley and Cole remain frozen in place as Sasha bolts into the mist and vanishes. In a distance they hear him calling out for Igor—his shrill voice begging to be left alone from whatever he just encountered.

"What do you think just happened?"

Maxwell turns to look at Lincoln. He shrugs.

28

"I just thought you'd like to see this—Oscar-worthy movie if I do say so myself Todd dear—such excellent performances."

Todd Whitney glances at Lizette curiously as he looks at his hands still shackled with handcuffs. He seems enraged.

"You're a dead woman—you'll regret tangling with me bitch—I swear I'll crucify you—do you hear me *whore*."

Lizette wags her finger and laughs.

"This is the thanks I get for allowing you to have a movie to watch while you pass the time—such nerve—oh well."

She smirks and gives him a knowing look as she watches the screen on the wall suddenly come to life. She laughs slyly.

Page 138

"I think you'll recognize the stars of this movie. Both are making their film debuts—the first of many I assure you."

As the screen in front of him flickers Todd realizes what he's watching. As his daughter is raped several times by Anton it seems time stands still for Todd. Lizette laughs gleefully.

"Anton really enjoyed himself—blew his load plenty."

Lizette wags her finger at Todd once more.

"He wasn't wearing a condom in case you were wondering if he brought protection with him before he scored with your precious daughter. Oops—could a baby be on the way?"

She laughs again as she watches Todd clench his fist as he struggles against the confines of his handcuffs. He sighs.

"I'll kill you. I swear. I'll kill that bastard too if it's the last thing I do. I'll revel in his death right before I take Houghton Fawcett to hell with me. You're all gonna pay dearly."

Lizette begins laughing again.

"Oh—I'm so scared—such dramatics from a guy who's handcuffed and being held prisoner in the Fawcett mansion."

She points her finger at Todd.

"You're done—do you not understand that. Fawcett is calling the shots concerning your life now. One word from him and you're gonna end up at the bottom of San Francisco Bay."

Lizette leans toward Todd and smirks.

"If I were you I'd start wondering how Houghton plans to kill you—that man has a mean streak running through him."

She reaches out and grabs Todd by the neck.

"But most importantly think about what he has in store for you precious daughter—from student to prostitute—*oh my*."

She begins laughing and leaves the room.

29

"I think it's time we go away for the weekend."

Diane watches as her father comes toward her unaware of what she has planned for him. She nods several times and begins circling him. He doesn't notice that she seems oddly quiet.

Page **139**

"How about Seattle—Marko's family has a cabin there. It's right on Puget Sound—wonderful scenery—postcard perfect."

Eugene reacts to Marko's name being mentioned as Diane takes a step closer to her father. He seems irritated.

"Marko is old news Diane. You can do better than him. That Prinze boy had problems—he wasn't right for you."

Diane takes another step toward her father and gives him a cautious look as she slowly reaches into her jacket pocket.

"If he isn't—who is? Who should I date?"

Eugene seems annoyed and turns away briefly.

"Anyone but that Prinze boy—especially since he's sort of no longer in the picture—it seems he suddenly took a vacation."

Diane reacts as she looks at her father coldly. As he turns around a bullet lodges itself in his forehead. He falls backwards seconds later. Diane looks at the gun in her hand and sighs.

"You always said I should know how to use a gun if someone tried to hurt me daddy. I bet you never thought I'd use my training to put a bullet in your head for hurting Marko."

She looks at the gun in her hand again.

30
New Orleans

"What the fuck just happened? Did you see that?"

Lincoln turns to look at Wesley and Cole as they continue looking at the mist expecting to see Igor and Sasha return.

"I think one of those dead people buried in the cemetery on this property made their presence known. It's either that or those two bozos faked everything—played us for fools."

Parker wags his finger at Lincoln.

"That's the dumbest thing I ever heard."

Lincoln rolls his eyes.

"Uh-huh—yeah I'm an idiot—this from the guy who said he saw several people turn to mush right before his eyes."

Parker jabs Lincoln and faces the others.

"I have no idea what he's talking about—he lies."

Maxwell watches the reactions of Wesley and Cole and faces Lincoln again. He runs his fingers through his hair.

"Well, how about that key? Cough it up."

Lincoln shoots Maxwell a look of disdain. He shuffles his feet a bit and turns to look at David and Parker. They sigh.

"Just give it to him already and let's get the hell out of this place—I'm done—finished—worse than a horror movie."

Lincoln stares at David for a few seconds and reaches for the skeleton key in the back pocket of his Levi's as a hush comes over the area. Everyone notices. The stillness is palpable.

"I've changed my mind."

At that moment the skeleton key in Lincoln's hand begins melting. He reacts and drops the key as it continues to lose its shape and become a blob of melted metal. Lincoln seems confused as it suddenly bursts into flames and disintegrates into dust. Lincoln turns to look at Maxwell in shock and then faces the ash pile in front of him that had once been a skeleton key.

"Did you see that? What the fuck?"

Brian shakes his head briefly and bursts out laughing as he faces Lincoln. He snaps his fingers several times nervously.

"OK—OK—this is too fucked up to be real. Seriously, how did you do that? This is the coolest magic trick ever—twisted."

Lincoln glances at Parker and then stares at Brian.

"You think this was a frigging magic trick?"

Brian shoots Lincoln a sharp look.

"Wasn't it?"

Lincoln shakes his head.

"It wasn't me."

Maxwell hears a sound and turns to see Tiffany standing less than two feet away. She points and begins laughing.

31

Police cars blanket the parking lot in front of a police station as Diane walks toward the entrance. She seems upset as she reaches for the doorknob and several people notice her.

Page **141**

32

"Are you nuts? There are no such things as ghosts. You imagined the whole thing—created whatever you saw."

Houghton Fawcett paces around his office.

"I want that frigging key. I don't want to hear about your ludicrous ravings anymore. Go back and get it—*or else.*"

He slams his cell phone down in a rage.

33
New Orleans

"He didn't believe us—said we made it up—said he wanted that key or else—didn't say what he meant by the way."

Igor watches Sasha's reaction and sighs loudly as they seem in shock as they stand in a deserted parking lot.

"It was real. That teenage boy was real. He grabbed me just as I said—felt like an electric shock. Told me he was gonna kill me—said I'd crossed the wrong person—and then he turned into a frigging skeleton. Laughed as he said it was my time."

Igor runs his fingers through his hair.

"The girl said the same thing—warned me that scary things were on their way as she turned into a skeleton too."

They look toward the abandoned estate in a distance and shudder as they seem to remember the moment they came in contact with the teen specters. Igor shakes his head.

"I'm not going back there."

Sasha shoots Igor a cautious look.

34
London

Dirk looks at a photograph of **Henry Morgan** on a website detailing his criminal history. He shakes his head and seems a bit confused as he leans closer to the huge computer screen.

Page **142**

"No wonder so many bad things befell Jim Hawkins after he acquired Morgan's ill-gotten treasure. It was cursed—cursed all those who came in contact with it—destroyed lives."

He turns away from the computer.

"No wonder it was hidden away somewhere in New Orleans by one of my distant relatives during the nineteenth century. They must have found out the awful truth and wanted Morgan's treasure to remain lost forever—never to be found."

He glances at his cell phone and reaches for it.

35
New Orleans

Maxwell closes the door to his hotel room as his cell phone begins to ring. He looks at the name on the screen and winces.

"I guess he knows what happened already."

He clicks on the name and seconds later Dirk appears on screen. He seems upset about something. Maxwell sighs.

"Hello Dirk—I was expecting your call. I guess you spoke to William already and heard what happened earlier."

Dirk seems confused and grimaces.

"I haven't spoken to William yet. I'm calling about the treasure. I know who it really belonged to—plenty drama."

Maxwell reacts in shock as he's told about the origins of the elusive treasure and almost stumbles. He regains his step.

36

Houghton seems irritated as he looks at the cell phone on his desk. He clenches his fist and seems enraged. He grimaces.

"I've waited too long to get my hands on Morgan's treasure—killed too many people to achieve my goal."

He begins laughing as he looks at the phone again. As he leans back in his chair he realizes he's no longer alone in his office as a thick mist begins forming. Seconds later Tiffany stands before him. They lock eyes as he sits up. She beckons him.

"How did you get into my office?"

Tiffany takes a step forward. Houghton reaches for his gun as Tiffany laughs. As he watches in shock the gun falls from his hand and bursts into flames. He reacts as she points at him.

"*You've been marked.*"

Seconds later she's gone. Houghton remains frozen and seems unable to move. He looks around his office but sees no one else in the room with him. He finally takes a deep breath.

"What the fuck was that?"

Houghton glances at the melted blob that was his gun seconds earlier and realizes it's nothing but a pile of dust now.

37
New Orleans

Maxwell takes another swig from the beer in his hand and seems unaware of his surroundings. He looks at the cell phone lying nearby and shakes his head several times. Behind him he notices a movement in the mirror and turns to see Tiffany staring back at him. She seems pleased with herself and laughs.

"How was the show earlier—did it impress?"

Maxwell runs his fingers through his hair and sighs.

"Where is Morgan's treasure?"

Tiffany waves her hand in the air and grins.

"It's where it should be."

Maxwell seems annoyed.

"What's that supposed to mean?"

Tiffany takes a step forward.

"That treasure has brought everyone who came in contact with it nothing but tragedy. The *key* was its last link—now there's no key—gone—*poof*. That wretched treasure is forever lost."

Maxwell shoots Tiffany a cautious look.

"You know where it is—don't you?"

Tiffany begins laughing and seems amused.

"Duh—of course—what do you think?"

She takes another step toward Maxwell and smirks.

"It'll never be found—not by anyone alive anyway. I made sure of that—with a little help from Jim Hawkins of course."

As he watches in stunned amazement Maxwell realizes someone else is standing besides Tiffany—a young man dressed in clothing reminiscent of the eighteenth century. He and Maxwell look at each other for a few seconds and then he vanishes as quickly as he appeared. Tiffany gestures briefly.

"In case you were wondering—no one else saw me but you and those two idiot Russian morons. They got quite a scare."

Tiffany wags her finger at Maxwell and laughs slyly as she takes another step forward. They silently look at each other for a few seconds and then she's gone as if she was never there.

One Day Later

38

Houghton watches the television screen in front of him as troubling news concerning the death of Marko Prinze—of which the connected deaths of Bruce Copeland and Eugene Singer creates a field day for the local media as cameras are shoved in more than one person's face. He grimaces as he turns to look at his office. He takes another swig of his drink and sighs loudly.

TO BE CONTINUED

A Brief Look at the Final Episode

Certain events continue to haunt those left behind after the terrifying incident in New Orleans unraveled while loose ends are tied up for more than one person in ways they never expected.

Episode 6
Out of the Shadows

1

"I know what I saw—this *thing*—this *creature*—was as real as you and I am right now. That bitch threatened me—said I was marked—left me to wonder what she meant—laughed."

Loren Fawcett shakes his head and leans back in his chair as his father walks back and forth in front of his desk.

"What do you want me to say? I don't have an answer for you—it sounds like something right out of **Amityville**."

Houghton Fawcett faces his son and sighs.

"Do you think this is some sort of a joke? People said *that* story was bogus—said it was made it up—but no one could explain the photo taken a year after the story broke of a little boy standing at the foot of a staircase in the house. It was said that he resembled the youngest of the murder victims killed in 1974."

Loren runs his fingers through his hair.

"What does that have to do with what you said happened to you yesterday? You said you didn't recognize her."

Loren stands and slowly walks over to where his father is standing. He notices his father's odd behavior and sighs.

Page **147**

"Maybe you should take a vacation. Go to Fiji for a few weeks. Forget about this ghost nonsense and get some rest."

Houghton clenches his fist in anger.

"I won't let that *thing* work her magic on me. I'll kill her first—destroy her. I swear I'll break her like I've done others."

Loren gives Houghton a cautious look.

"I think it's time you pay Carlisle McMarland a visit. I'm sure he'll see you on short notice. How about it? Should I call?"

Houghton slams his fist against Loren's jaw.

2

Marble Hills

Maxwell Pendergraft watches as Eddie Kane closes the door behind him. He acknowledges Gina Bentley as he walks toward a chair a few feet away. He seems tired. They notice.

"Did she say anything else?"

Maxwell turns to face Eddie and sighs.

"Nothing other than what she told me when she made her presence known. It was weird seeing her again—strange."

Gina shoots Eddie a curious look and shrugs.

"I haven't seen Tiffany Johnson since Jennifer Parker died. I thought when the school was finished she'd pay me a visit—but there's been no contact. Not with me or with anyone else."

Maxwell runs his fingers through his hair.

"She wasn't alone. Jeremy Weissmann was with her."

Eddie and Gina both react in shock.

"Did anyone else see them?"

Maxwell runs his fingers through his hair again.

"Two Russian thugs apparently from what she told me afterwards—said she and Jeremy gave them quite a scare."

Maxwell laughs at the memory.

"She seemed quite pleased with herself when we talked and seemed to enjoy the power she now held—relished it."

Eddie glances at Gina and faces Maxwell again.

"What about the treasure chest?"

Page **148**

Maxwell glances at Eddie briefly and sighs.

"From what I know it once belonged to **Henry Morgan** and was hidden somewhere in New Orleans by the relatives of a long-dead British man who found it on a voyage to the West Indies during his youth. A missing key then set in motion a murderous rampage orchestrated by a ruthless Russian mob family based in California which then culminated in New Orleans where Tiffany made her presence known to yours truly."

He tries to stifle a laugh.

"It was something to see I assure you."

Maxwell rubs his eyes and faces them again.

"Seemed like a movie."

Eddie and Gina look at each other briefly.

3

"This can't be happening to me—*to Lincoln.*"

Stanley Ross turns to face his son and seems annoyed. He sighs as he watches Roosevelt Ross looking at the doorway.

"It's gone—all of it. I owe everyone money."

He walks toward his son.

"I already spoke to your mother—you can stay with her until I figure things out. She's waiting for your call son."

Roosevelt looks at his father and shrugs.

"I don't want to be poor."

Stanley grabs his cell phone.

"That makes two of us."

Roosevelt rolls his eyes and turns away.

4

"Did you see how those guys freaked out at that old estate in New Orleans? Acted like they saw a ghost or something? It was like *so* right out of *Comes the Blind Fury* by **John Saul.**"

David Sherwood shoots Lincoln Ross an odd look and sighs. Lincoln notices and waves his hand in the air and laughs.

Page 149

"It was a really good novel. I guess you don't read."

Parker Ross slaps David in the back and grins.

"Seriously, the only thing David Sherwood reads is the names in his little black book. He's got all his conquests listed by how good they were between the sheets. This dude even has an image of an ugly turkey near the ones that disappointed him."

David shoves Parker playfully.

"It must really hurt to be you—tragically lame with girls."

Parker reacts and begins laughing.

"Ouch—terribly cruel buddy—even for you."

They pretend to shadow box as Lincoln looks at his cell phone and sees his father on the other end. He grimaces.

5

New Orleans

Anton Levitov looks at William La Porte for a few seconds as he smashes his fist again his jaw. He seems enraged.

"Where is that fucking treasure?"

William wipes blood from his lips and shakes his head. He seems confused as he watches Anton clench his fist.

"I already told you I don't know where it's hidden. The key was destroyed—something happened to it—it burned up."

"In that case I guess there's no reason for me not to make good on the promise I made to you previous. Time's up."

He licks his lips several times. Less than a second later he shoots William in the chest at point-blank range. The frightened man screams only once as he falls backwards. Anton laughs.

"I always make good on my promises."

He smirks as he closes the front door of William's house behind him and begins walking down the sidewalk to his car.

6

"I already told you—he's gone off the deep end—keeps saying something about a teenage girl threatening him."

Page **150**

Loren turns to look at Vladimir Orlov and sighs.

"I think it's best if I take over running the business for now. A few days in Fiji might provide much needed rest for him."

Vladimir winks at Loren and wags his finger.

"Uh-huh—I see where this is going. You're wresting control from the old man. Uh-huh—slick move no doubt."

Loren seems insulted and turns away.

"How dare you suggest I would do such a thing?"

Vladimir takes a step forward.

"Don't pretend with me—I know exactly what you're up to cousin—facts are facts. The old man has seen better days."

Loren faces Vladimir and grins broadly.

7

Houghton reacts as he sees a teenage girl staring back at him from a huge mirror in his bedroom. He begins screaming and grabs a large vase—throwing it toward the mirror. Seconds later the teenage girl appears inches away from him. She grins.

8

New York City

Scott Malone looks at headlines detailing the demise of Stanley Ross and his business empire. He seems upset as he puts the newspaper on top of a coffee table as Sandra King comes toward him from the patio with a copy of her manuscript.

About the Series Creator

Gary Brin was born in 1965 and has lived in the United States Virgin Islands, Hawaii and California. He has edited numerous original literary works over the years—both new and revised. In 2019 he established Standish Press to bring forth interesting fictional and historical material usually ignored by mainstream publishers because of specific views or content. In addition to publishing books, he also created the Nancy Hanks Lincoln Public Library (named after the mother of Abraham Lincoln) in 2014 to make available hard-to-find books to a worldwide audience.

Production Notes

Written by Wesley Adams and Daphne McGee
Manuscript edited by Gary Brin
Cover photograph from www.pexels.com
Front cover design and interior book layout by Gary Brin
Cover layout by Victoria Valentine
Additional help provided by Carlton J. Young
Series created by Gary Brin

Character List

Steve Andersen
Reginald Balding
Sherry Barnes
Tammy Barnes
Gina Bentley
John Berringer
Carla Bington
Scott Bington
Hugh Blandwick
Cole Bouvier
Pierce Colby
Bruce Copeland
Brian Delgado
Tiffany Dennington
Houghton Fawcett
Loren Fawcett
Tyler Fields
Jared Goulet
Dirk Hawkins
Evelyn Hayes
Tiffany Johnson
Eddie Kane
Sandra King
Kevin Kulkovich
William La Porte
Anton Levitov
Igor Levitov
Sasha Levitov
Carol Malinger
Christian Malinger
Jesse Malinger
Juliet Malinger

Scott Malone
Lorraine McCall
Cujo Momoa
Lance Moon
Sergei Orlov
Vladimir Orlov
Roland Parker
Maxwell Pendergraft
Marko Prinze
Lizette Richardson
Irving Rivera
Lincoln Ross
Parker Ross
Roosevelt Ross
Stanley Ross
Veronica Ross
Adam Sanchez
Marisa Sanz
David Sherwood
Diane Singer
Eugene Singer
Erik Smith
Harcourt Styverson
Travis Sweeney
Wesley Trudeau
Jeremy Weissmann
Bridget Whitney
Todd Whitney
Chad Winchester

Real People Mentioned

Tonya Crowe
Donna Mills
Henry Morgan
John Saul
Tammy Wynette

Next in the Series
Book 7
Ocean Landing
Dangerous Games

9 781945 510076